The Billionaire's Borrowed Baby

JANICE MAYNARD

First published in Great Britain 2012
by Mills & Boon, an imprint of Harlequin (UK) Limited.
Large Print edition 2012
Harlequin (UK) Limited,
Eton House, 18-24 Paradise Road,
Richmond, Surrey TW9 1SR

© Janice Maynard 2011

ISBN: 978 0 263 22969 1

Harlequin (UK) policy is to use papers that are natural, renewable and recyclable products and made from wood grown in sustainable forests. The logging and manufacturing process conform to the legal environmental regulations of the country of origin.

Printed and bound in Great Britain
by CPI Antony Rowe, Chippenham, Wiltshire

"Tell me, Hattie. What do you want?"

She lifted her chin. She was tall for a woman, and he could see the shades of chocolate and cognac in her pupils. She licked her lips. Their long separation vanished like mist, and suddenly he was assaulted with a barrage of memories, both good and bad.

The soft, quick kiss he brushed across her cheek surprised them both. He was so close, he could smell cherry lipgloss. Some things never changed. "Hattie?"

She closed her eyes when he kissed her, but her lashes lifted and her cloudy gaze cleared. Astonishment flashed across her expressive features, followed by chagrin and what appeared to be resignation.

After a long, silent pause, she wrinkled her nose and sighed. "I need you to marry me."

Dear Reader,

I am married to a man who much prefers the mountains to the beach but who also loves Key West! We have made several trips down to the jewel-like islands that make up the tip of Florida, sometimes flying straight in and sometimes landing in Ft. Lauderdale and renting a car to drive down the Keys.

When I began to think of a fun destination that met certain requirements for Luc and Hattie's unconventional honeymoon, I knew that Key West would be a perfect locale. It has everything—fabulous weather, a colourful, original ambience, loads of history (everything from pirates to Hemingway), and undoubtedly— romance!

Two people who have joined forces for the sake of a child may try fooling themselves into thinking the marriage is in name only. But beneath a tropical moon, surrounded by scented breezes and centuries of swashbuckling adventure, Luc and Hattie can't resist revisiting the love they once shared.

Happy reading,

Janice

JANICE MAYNARD

came to writing early in life. When her short story *The Princess and the Robbers* won a red ribbon in her primary school arts fair, Janice was hooked. She holds a B.A. from Emory and Henry College and an M.A. from East Tennessee State University. In 2002 Janice left a fifteen-year career as an elementary teacher to pursue writing full-time. Her first love is creating sexy, character-driven, contemporary romance. She has written for Kensington and NAL, and now is so very happy to also be part of the Mills & Boon family—a lifelong dream, by the way!

Janice and her husband live in beautiful east Tennessee in the shadow of the Great Smoky Mountains. She loves to travel and enjoys using those experiences as settings for books.

Hearing from readers is one of the best perks of the job! Visit her website at www.janicemaynard.com or e-mail her at JESM13@aol.com. And of course, don't forget Facebook (www.facebook.com/JaniceMaynardReaderPage). Find her on Twitter at www.twitter.com/

For the next generation: Anastasia, Ainsley, Allie, Sydney, Olivia, Dakota and Samuel Ellis.

One

It was a hot, beautiful Georgia morning, but all Hattie Parker noticed was the taste of desperation and panic.

"I need to speak to Mr. Cavallo, please. Mr. *Luc* Cavallo," she clarified quickly. "It's urgent."

The thirtysomething administrative assistant with the ice-blue suit and matching pale, chilly eyes looked down her perfect nose. "Do you have an appointment?"

Hattie clenched her teeth. The woman had an expensive leather date book open in front of her. Clearly, she knew Hattie was an interloper and clearly she was doing her best to be intimidating.

Hattie juggled the baby on her hip and managed

a smile. "Tell him it's Hattie Parker. I don't have an appointment, but I'm sure Luc will see me if you let him know I'm here."

Actually, that was a bald-faced lie. She had no clue if Luc would see her or not. At one time in her life he had been Prince Charming, willing and eager to do anything she wanted, to give her everything she desired.

Today, he might very well show her the door, but she was hoping he would remember some of the good times and at least hear her out. They hadn't parted on the best of terms. But since every other option she had considered, legal or not, had gone bust, it was Luc or no one. And she wasn't leaving without a fight.

The woman's expression didn't change. She was sheer perfection from her ash-blond chignon to her exquisitely made-up face to her expensive French manicure. With disdain, she examined Hattie's disheveled blond hair, discount store khaki skirt and pink cotton blouse. Even without the drool marks at the shoulder, the outfit wasn't going to win any fashion awards. It was hard to maintain a neat appearance when the little one grabbed handfuls of hair at regular intervals.

Hattie's legs felt like spaghetti. The stoic security guard in the lobby had insisted that she park her stroller before entering the elevator. Seven-month-old Deedee weighed a ton, and Hattie was scared and exhausted, at the end of her rope. The last six weeks had been hell.

She took a deep breath. "Either you let me see Mr. Cavallo, or I'm going to pitch the biggest hissy fit Atlanta has seen since Scarlett O'Hara swished her skirts through the red Georgia dust." Hattie's chin trembled right at the end, but she refused to let this supercilious woman defeat her.

Scary lady blinked. Just once, but it was enough to let Hattie know that the balance of power had shifted. The other woman stood up with a pained sigh. "Wait here." She disappeared down a hallway.

Hattie nuzzled the baby's sweet-smelling head with its little tufts of golden hair. "Don't worry, my love. I won't let anyone take you, I swear." Deedee smiled, revealing her two new bottom teeth, her only teeth. She was starting to babble nonsense syllables, and Hattie fell more in love with her every day.

The wait seemed like an eternity, but when

Luc's assistant finally returned, the clock on the wall showed that less than five minutes had elapsed. The woman was definitely disgruntled. "Mr. Cavallo will see you now. But he's a very busy man, and he has many other important commitments this morning."

Hattie resisted the childish urge to stick out her tongue at the woman's back as they traversed the hallway carpeted in thick, crimson plush. At the second doorway, the woman paused. "You may go in." The words nearly stuck in ice woman's throat, you could tell.

Hattie took a deep breath, no longer concentrating on her would-be nemesis. She kissed the baby's cheek for luck. "Showtime, kiddo." With far more confidence than she felt, she knocked briefly, opened the door and stepped into the room.

Luc ran a multimillion-dollar business. He was accustomed to dealing with crises on a daily basis. The ability to think on his feet was a gift he'd honed in the fires of corporate America.

So he wasn't easily thrown off balance. But when Hattie Parker appeared in his office, the first time he'd seen her in over a decade, his heart lodged in his throat, his muscles tensed and he momentarily forgot how to breathe.

She was as beautiful now as she had been at twenty. Sun-kissed porcelain skin, dark brown eyes that held hints of amber. And legs that went on forever. Her silky blond hair barely brushed her shoulders, much shorter than he remembered. He kept the width of his broad mahogany desk between them. It seemed safer that way.

As he struggled with shock, he was stunned to realize the woman he had once loved was holding an infant. Jealousy stabbed sharp and deep. Damn. Hattie was a mother. Which meant there was a man somewhere in the picture.

The sick feeling in his gut stunned him. He'd moved on a long, long time ago. So why was his chest tight and his pulse jumping like a jackrabbit?

He remained standing, his hands shoved in his pockets. "Hello, Hattie." He was proud of the even timbre of his voice.

"Hello, Luc."

She was visibly nervous. He indicated the chair closest to him and motioned for her to sit. For a brief moment, Luc caught a glimpse of sexy legs as Hattie's skirt rode up her thighs. The baby clung to her neck, and Hattie wriggled in the chair until she was modestly covered.

He examined her face, deliberately letting the silence accumulate in tense layers. Hattie Parker was the girl next door, a natural, appealing beauty who didn't need enhancement. Even dressed as she was in fairly unflattering garments, she would stand out in a room full of lovely women.

At one time, she had been his whole world.

And it irked him that the memories still stung. "Why are you here, Hattie? The last time we had sex was a lifetime ago. Surely you're not going to try and convince me that baby is mine."

The mockery and sarcasm made her pale. He felt the pinch of remorse, but a guy needed to wield what weapons he could. The man he was today would not be vulnerable. Not ever again.

She cleared her throat. "I need your help."

He lifted a brow. "I'd have thought I would be the last person on your go-to list."

"To be honest, you were. But it's serious, Luc. I'm in big trouble."

He rocked on his heels. "What's her name?"

The non sequitur made Hattie frown. "This is Deedee."

Luc studied the baby. He didn't see much of Hattie in the child. Maybe the kid took after her dad.

Luc leaned over and punched the intercom. "Marilyn…can you come in here, please?"

It was a toss-up as to which of the two women was more horrified when Luc phrased his next request. When Marilyn appeared, he motioned to the baby. "Will you please take the little one for a few minutes? Her name is Deedee. Ms. Parker and I need to have a serious conversation, and I don't have much time."

Hattie wanted to protest, he could tell. But she reluctantly handed the baby over to Luc's assistant. "Here's a bottle. She's getting hungry. And you'll need this bib and burp cloth. You don't want to let her ruin your nice suit."

Luc knew his assistant would be fine. She might be a cold fish, but she was relentlessly efficient.

When the door closed, Luc sat down in his leather office chair. It had been specially ordered to fit his long, lanky frame. He steepled his hands under his chin and leaned back. "So spill it, Hattie. What's going on in your life to make you seek me out? As I recall, it was *you* who dumped *me* and not the other way around."

She flushed and twisted her hands in her lap. "I don't think we need to go there. That was a long time ago."

He shrugged. "All right then. We'll concentrate on the present. Why are you here?"

When she bit her lip, he shifted in his chair uneasily. Why in God's name did he still have such vivid memories of kissing that bow-shaped mouth? Running his hands through that silky, wavy hair. Touching every inch of her soft, warm skin. He swallowed hard.

Hattie met his gaze hesitantly. "Do you remember my older sister, Angela?"

He frowned. "Barely. As I recall, the two of you didn't get along."

"We grew closer after our parents died."

"I didn't know, Hattie. I'm sorry."

For a moment, tears made her eyes shiny, but she blinked them back. "Thank you. My father died a few years after I graduated. Lung cancer.

He was a two-pack-a-day man and it caught up with him."

"And your mother?"

"She didn't do well without Daddy. He did everything for her, and without him, the world was overwhelming to her. She finally had a nervous breakdown and had to be admitted to a facility. Unfortunately, she was never able to go back to her home. Angela and I sold the house we grew up in…everything Mom and Dad had, but it wasn't enough. I practically bankrupted myself paying for her care."

"Angela didn't help?"

"She told me I should back off and let the state look after Mother…especially when Mom retreated totally into an alternate reality where she didn't even recognize us."

"Some people would think your sister made sense."

"Not me. I couldn't abandon my mother."

"When did you lose her?"

"Last winter."

He looked at her left hand, but it was bare. Where was her husband in all this? Was the guy a jerk who bailed on Hattie rather than help with the mom? And what about the baby?

Suddenly, it became clear. Hattie needed to borrow money. She was proud and independent, and things must be really bad if she had humbled her pride enough to come to him.

He leaned forward, his elbows on the desk. No one who knew their history would blame him if he kicked her out. But though his memories of her were bitter, he didn't have it in him to be deliberately cruel, especially if a child was involved. And though it might be petty, he rather liked the idea of having Hattie in his debt...a kind of poetic justice. "You've had a rough time," he said quietly. "I'll be happy to loan you however much money you need, interest free, no questions asked. For old time's sake."

Hattie's face went blank and she cocked her head. "Excuse me?"

"That's why you're here, isn't it? To ask if you can borrow some money? I'm fine with that. It's no big deal. What good is all that cash in the bank if I can't use it to help an old friend?"

Her jaw dropped and her cheeks went red with mortification. "No, no, no," she said, leaping to her feet and pacing. "I don't need your money, Luc. That's not it at all."

It was his turn to rise. He rounded the desk and faced her, close enough now to inhale her scent and realize with pained remembrance that she still wore the same perfume. He put his hands gently on her shoulders, feeling the tremors she couldn't disguise.

They were practically nose to nose. "Then tell me, Hattie. What do you need from me? What do you want?"

She lifted her chin. She was tall for a woman, and he could see the shades of chocolate and cognac in her irises. Her breathing was ragged, a pulse beating at the base of her throat.

He shook her gently. "Spit it out. Tell me."

She licked her lips. He could see the tracery of blue veins at her temples. Their long separation vanished like mist, and suddenly he was assaulted with a barrage of memories, both good and bad.

The soft, quick kiss he brushed across her cheek surprised them both. He was so close, he could smell cherry lip gloss. Some things never changed. "Hattie?"

She had closed her eyes when he kissed her, but her lashes lifted and her cloudy gaze cleared. Astonishment flashed across her expressive features, followed by chagrin and what appeared to be resignation.

After a long, silent pause, she wrinkled her nose and sighed. "I need you to marry me."

Luc dropped his hands from her shoulders with unflattering haste. Though his expression remained guarded, for a split second some strong emotion flashed in his eyes and then disappeared as quickly as it had come. Most men would be shocked by Hattie's proposal.

Most men weren't Luc Cavallo.

He lifted a shoulder clad in an expensive suit. The Cavallo textile empire, started by their grandfather in Italy and now headquartered in Atlanta, had made Luc and his brother wealthy men. She had no doubt that the soft, finely woven wool fabric was the product of a family mill. His mouth twisted, faint disdain in his expression. "Is this a joke? Should I look for hidden cameras?"

She felt her face go even hotter. Confronting her past was more difficult than she had expected, and without the baby to run interference, Hattie felt uncomfortably vulnerable. "It's not a joke. I'm dead serious. I need you to marry me to keep Deedee safe."

He scowled. "Good Lord, Hattie. Is the father threatening you? Has he hurt you? Tell me."

His intensity made her shiver. If she really had an abusive husband, there was no doubt in her mind that Luc Cavallo would hunt him down and destroy him. She was making a hash of this explanation. "It's complicated," she said helplessly. "But no, nothing like that."

He ran two hands through his hair, mussing the dark, glossy strands. The reminder function on his BlackBerry beeped just then, and Luc glanced down at it with a harried expression. "I have an appointment," he said, his voice betraying frustration. "Obviously we're not going to resolve this in fifteen minutes. Can you get a sitter for tonight?"

"I'd rather not. Deedee has been through a lot of trauma recently. She clings to me. I don't want to change her routine any more than necessary." And the thought of being alone with Luc Cavallo scared Hattie. This brief meeting had revealed an unpalatable truth. The Hattie who had been madly in love with Luc was still lurking somewhere inside a heart that clung to silly dreams from the past.

He straightened his tie and strode to the other side of his desk. "Then I'll send a car for you." As she opened her mouth to protest, he added, "With an infant seat. We'll have dinner at my home and my housekeeper can play with the child while we talk."

There was nothing ominous in his words, but Hattie felt her throat constrict. Was she really going to try to convince Luc to marry her? Who was she kidding? He had no reason at all to humor her. Other than perhaps sheer curiosity. Why hadn't he shown her the door immediately? Why was he allowing her to play out this odd reunion?

She should be glad, relieved, down on her knees thanking the good lord that Luc wasn't already married.

But at the moment, her exact emotions were far more complicated and far less sensible.

She was still fascinated by this man who had once promised her the moon.

Two

What did one wear to a marriage proposal? While the baby was napping, Hattie rummaged through the tiny closet in her matching tiny apartment, knowing that she was not going to find a dress to wow Luc Cavallo. The only garment remotely suitable was a black, polished cotton sheath that she had worn to each of her parent's funerals. Perhaps with some accessories it would do the trick.

In a jewelry box she'd had since she was a girl, her hand hovered over the one piece inside that wasn't an inexpensive bauble. The delicate platinum chain was still as bright as the day Luc had given it to her. She picked it up and fastened it around her neck, adjusting the single pearl flanked by small diamonds.

Though there had been many days when the wolf was at the door, she had not been able to bring herself to sell this one lovely reminder of what might have been. She stroked the pearl, imagining that it was warm beneath her fingers.…

They had skipped their afternoon classes at Emory and escaped to Piedmont Park with a blanket and a picnic basket. She was a scholarship student…his family had endowed the Fine Arts Center.

As they sprawled in the hot spring sunshine, feeling alive and free and deliciously truant, Luc leaned over her on one elbow, kissing her with teasing brushes of his lips that made her restless for more. He grinned down at her, his eyes alight with happiness. "I have an anniversary present for you."

"Anniversary?" They'd been dating for a while, but she hadn't kept track.

He caressed her cheek. "I met you six months ago today. You were buying a miniature pumpkin at *Stanger's Market. I offered to carve it for you. You laughed. And that's when I knew."*

"Knew what?"

"That you were the one."

Her smile faded. "College guys are supposed to be counting notches on their bedposts, not spouting romantic nonsense."

A shadow dimmed the good humor in his gaze. "I come from a long line of Italians. Romance is in our blood." His whimsical shrug made her regret tarnishing the moment. Lord knew she wanted it to be true, but her mother had drummed into her head that men only wanted one thing. And Hattie had given that up without a qualm.

Being Luc Cavallo's lover was the best thing that had ever happened to her. He was her first, and she loved him so much it hurt. But she was careful to protect herself. She had a degree to finish, grades to keep up. A woman had to stand on her own two feet. Depending on a man led to heartbreak.

Luc reached into the pocket of his jeans and withdrew a small turquoise box. He handed it to her without speaking.

If she had been able to think of a polite refusal,

she would have handed it back unopened. But he looked at her with such naked anticipation that she swallowed her misgivings and removed the lid. Nestled inside the leather box was a necklace, an exquisite, expensive necklace.

Hattie knew about Tiffany's, of course. In fact, back in the fall she'd been in the store at Phipps Plaza with one of her girlfriends who was in search of a wedding gift. But even on that day, Hattie had felt the sting of being out of place. She couldn't afford a key chain in those swanky glass cases, much less anything else.

And now this.

Luc ignored her silence. He took the necklace from the box and fastened it around her neck. She was wearing a pink tank top, and the pearl nestled in her modest cleavage. He kissed her forehead. "It suits you."

But it didn't. She was not that woman he wanted her to be. Luc would take his place one day with the glitterati. And Hattie, with or without the necklace, would wish him well. But she wasn't "the one"...and she never would be.

A car backfired out on the street, the loud sound dragging Hattie back to the present. With a mutinous scowl at her own reflection, she closed the jewelry box with a defiant click. Luc probably didn't even remember the silly necklace. He'd no doubt bought pricey bling for a dozen women in the intervening years.

The afternoon dragged by, the baby fussy with teething…Hattie nervous and uncertain. It was almost a relief when a nicely dressed chauffeur knocked at the door promptly at six-thirty.

The pleasant older man took Hattie's purse and the diaper bag while she tucked Deedee into the top-of-the-line car seat. It was brand-new and not smeared with crusty Cheerios and spit-up. The baby was charmed by the novelty of having Hattie sit across from her. A game of peekaboo helped distract them both as the car wound its way from the slightly run-down neighborhood where Hattie lived to an upscale part of town.

Though it had been ten years since Hattie and Luc's college breakup, they had never crossed paths after graduation. It was a big city, and they moved in far different spheres.

West Paces Ferry was one of the premier addresses in Atlanta. Decades-old homes sat side by side with new construction created to resemble historic architecture. Even the governor's man-sion called the narrow, winding avenue home. Luc had recently purchased an entire estate com-plete with acreage. Hattie had seen the renovation written up in a local magazine.

The article, accompanied by photos of Luc, had no doubt been responsible for this crazy deci-sion to throw herself on Luc's mercy. Seeing his smiling face after so many years had resurrected feelings she believed to be long dead.

Perhaps it was a sign.…

The old home was amazing. Azaleas and for-sythia bloomed in profusion on the grounds. A lengthy driveway culminated in a cobblestone apron leading to the imposing double front doors. Luc stepped out to meet them almost before the engine noise had died. His dark hair and eyes betrayed his Mediterranean heritage.

He held out a hand. "Welcome, Hattie."

She felt him squeeze her fingers, and her skin heated. "Your home is beautiful."

He stepped back as she extracted Deedee. "It's a work in progress. I'll be glad when the last of it is finished."

Despite his disclaimer, and despite the small

area of scaffolding at the side of the house where workmen had been repairing stonework, the interior of the house was breathtaking. A sweeping staircase led up and to the right. The foyer floor was Italian marble, and above a walnut chair rail, the walls were papered in what appeared to be the original silk fabric, a muted shade of celadon. A priceless chandelier showered them in shards of warm light, and on a console beneath an antique mirror on the left wall, a massive bouquet of flowers scented the air.

Hattie turned around in a circle, the baby in her arms quiet for once, as if she, too, was awed. "It's stunning, Luc."

His smile reflected quiet satisfaction. "It's starting to feel like home. The couple who lived here bought it in the 1920s. They're both gone now, but I inherited Ana and Sherman. He wears many hats…driver is only one of them."

"He was very sweet. I felt pampered. And Ana?"

"His wife. You'll meet her in a moment. She's the housekeeper, chef, gardener…you name it. I tried to get them both to retire with a pension, but I think they love this house more than I do.

I get the distinct feeling that I'm on probation as the new owner."

As promised, Ana entertained Deedee during dinner while Luc and Hattie enjoyed the fruits of the housekeeper's labors—lightly breaded rainbow trout, baby asparagus and fruit salad accompanied by rolls so fluffy they seemed to melt in the mouth.

Luc served Hattie and himself, with nothing to disturb the intimacy of their meal. Surprisingly, Hattie forgot to be self-conscious. Luc was a fascinating man, highly intelligent, well-read, and he possessed of a sneaky sense of humor. As the evening progressed, sharp regret stabbed her heart. She was overwhelmed with a painful recognition of what she had lost because of her own immaturity and cowardice.

He refilled her wineglass one more time. "I suppose you're not nursing the baby."

She choked on a sip of chardonnay. An image of Luc in her bed, watching her feed a baby at her breast, flashed through her brain with the force of a runaway train. Her face was so hot she hoped he would blame it on the wine. She set the glass down gently, her hand trembling. Unwittingly, he had given her the perfect opening.

"The baby's not mine," she said softly. "My sister Angela was her mother."

"Was?"

Hattie swallowed, the grief still fresh and raw. "She was killed in a car crash six weeks ago. My brother-in-law, Eddie, was driving...drunk and drugged out of his mind. He got out and left the scene when he hit a car head-on. Both people in the other vehicle died. Angela lingered for a few hours...long enough to tell me that she wanted me to take Deedee. I was babysitting that night, and I've had the baby ever since."

"What happened to the baby's father?"

"Eddie spent a few days behind bars. He's out on bail awaiting trial. But I guarantee you he won't do any time. His family has connections everywhere. I don't know if we have the Mob in Georgia, but I wouldn't be surprised. Eddie's family is full of cold, mean-spirited people. Frankly, they scare me."

"I can tell."

"At first, none of them showed any sign of acknowledging Deedee's existence. But about two

weeks ago, I was summoned to the family com-
pound in Conyers."

"Eddie wanted to see his child?"

She laughed bitterly. "You'd think so, wouldn't
you? But no. He was there when I arrived with
her. A lot of them were there. But not one single
person in that entire twisted family even looked
at her, much less asked to hold her. They kept
referring to her as 'the kid' and talked about how
she was one of theirs and so should be raised by
them."

"That doesn't make any sense given their lack
of enthusiasm for the baby."

"It does when you realize that Eddie thinks
Deedee will be his ace in the hole with the judge.
He wants to portray the grieving husband and
penitent dad. Having Deedee in the courtroom
will soften him, make him more sympathetic to
the jury."

"Ah. I take it you didn't go along with their
plan?"

"Of course not. I told them Angela wanted me
to raise her daughter and that I would be adopt-
ing Deedee."

"How did that go?"

She shivered. "Eddie's father said that no custody court would give a baby to a single woman with few financial means when the father wanted the child and had the resources to provide for her future."

"And you said…?"

She bit her lip. "I told them I was engaged to my college sweetheart and that you had a boatload of money and you loved Deedee like your own. And then I hightailed it out of there."

Luc actually had the gall to laugh.

"It's not funny," she wailed, leaping to her feet. "This is serious."

He topped off her wineglass once again. "Relax, Hattie. I have more lawyers than a dog has fleas. Deedee is safe. I give you my word."

Her legs went weak and she plopped into her chair. "Really? You mean that?" Suspicion reared its ugly head. "Why?"

He leaned back, studying her with a laserlike gaze that made her want to hide. He saw too much. "My motivation shouldn't matter…right, Hattie? If I really am your last resort?" Something in his bland words made her shiver.

She licked her lips, feeling as if she was making

a bargain with the devil. "Are you sure you're willing to do this?"

"I never say anything I don't mean. You should know that. We'll make your lie a reality. I have the best legal counsel in Atlanta. Angela's wishes will prevail."

"I'll sign a prenup," she said. "I don't want your money."

His gaze iced over. "You made that clear a decade ago, Hattie. No need to flog a dead horse."

Her stomach clenched. Why was it that he could make her feel so small with one look?

When she remained silent, he stood up with visible impatience. "I know you need to get the little one in bed before it gets any later. I'll have my team draw up some documents, and then in a few days, you and I can go over the details."

"Details?" she asked weakly.

His grin was feral. "Surely you know I'll have a few stipulations of my own."

Her throat tightened and she took one last swallow of wine. It burned going down like it was whiskey. "Of course. You have to protect your interests. That makes sense." For some reason she couldn't quite fathom, the specter of sex had unexpectedly entered the room. Her mouth was so dry she could barely speak.

Surely lawyers didn't use legalese to dictate sex...did they?

Suddenly an unpalatable thought struck her. "Um...Luc...I should have asked. Is there anyone who will... I mean...who is...um..."

He cocked his head, one broad shoulder propped against the door frame. His face was serious, but humor danced in his eyes. "Are you asking if I'm seeing anyone, Hattie? Isn't it a bit late to worry about that...now that you've told everyone I'm your fiancé?"

Mortified didn't begin to describe how she felt. "Not everyone," she muttered.

"Just the Mob?" He chuckled out loud, enjoying her discomfiture a little too much. Finally, he sobered. "You let me worry about my personal life, Hattie. Your job is to take care of yourself and that little girl—" He stopped abruptly. "Speaking of jobs...what happened? Why aren't you teaching?" She had majored in math at Emory and had gone directly from college to a high school faculty position.

"I had to take a leave of absence for the rest of the year when the accident happened."

He sobered completely now, stepping close enough to run a hand over her hair. She'd worn it loose tonight. "You've been through a hell of a lot," he said softly, their bodies almost touching. "But things will get better."

She smiled wistfully. "Somedays it seems as if nothing will ever be the same."

"I didn't say it would be the same."

For some reason, the words struck her as a threat. She looked up at him, their breath mingling. "What do you get out of this? Why did you agree to back up an impulsive lie by a woman you haven't seen in ten years?"

"Are you trying to talk me out of it?"

"Tell me why you agreed. I was ninety percent sure you'd throw me out of your office on my fanny."

"I can be kind on occasion." The sarcasm was impossible to miss.

She searched his face. It hurt knowing that it was as familiar to her as if they had parted yesterday. "There's something more," she said slowly. "I can see it in your eyes."

His expression shuttered. "Let's just say I have my reasons." His tone was gruff and said more loudly than words that he was done with the conversation.

He was shutting her out. And it stung. But they were little more than strangers now. Strangers who had once made love with passionate abandon, but strangers nevertheless.

"I have to go."

He didn't argue. He ushered her in front of him until they entered a pleasant room outfitted as a den. Ana, despite her years, was down on an Oriental rug playing with a sleepy Deedee.

Hattie rushed forward to scoop up the drowsy baby and nuzzle her sweet-smelling neck. "Did she nap for you at all?"

Ana stood with dignity and straightened the skirt of her floral cotton housedress. "She slept about forty-five minutes…enough to keep her awake until you can get her home and in bed. Your daughter is precious, Ms. Parker, an absolute angel."

"She's not my daughter, she's my niece…but thank you." Did the housekeeper think Luc had brought his love child home for a visit?

Her host grew impatient with the female chit-chat. "I'll walk you out, Hattie."

Sherman waited respectfully by the car door, making any sort of personal conversation awkward. Luc surprised Hattie by taking Deedee without ceremony and tucking her expertly into the small seat.

She lifted an eyebrow. "You did that well."

He touched the baby's cheek and stepped aside so Hattie could enter the limo. "It's not rocket science." He braced an arm on the top of the car and leaned in. "I'll look forward to seeing you both again soon."

"You'll call me?"

"I'll get Marilyn to contact you and set up a meeting. It will probably only take a couple of days. You need to go ahead and start packing."

"Packing?" She was starting to sound like a slightly dense parrot. What had she gotten herself into? Luc was helping her, but with strings attached. She had known his every thought at one time. Now he was an enigma.

His half smile made her think of a predator anticipating his prey. "You and Deedee will be moving in here as soon as the wedding is over."

Three

Two days later, Luc tapped briefly at his brother's office door and entered. Leo, his senior by little more than a year, was almost hidden behind piles of paperwork and books. A genius by any measure, Leo masterminded the financial empire, while Luc handled R & D. Luc enjoyed the challenge of developing new products, finding the next creative venture.

Leo was the one who made them all rich.

It was a full thirty seconds before his brother looked up from what he was doing. "Luc. Didn't expect to see you today."

The brothers met formally twice a month, and it wasn't unusual for them to lunch together a few times a week, but Luc rarely dropped by his brother's sanctum unannounced. Their offices were on different floors of the building, and more often than not, their customary mode of communication was texting.

Luc ignored the comfortable, overstuffed easy chair that flanked Leo's desk and instead, chose to cross the room and stand by the window. He never tired of gazing at Atlanta's distinctive skyline.

He rolled his shoulders, unaware until that moment that his neck was tight. He turned and smiled. "What are you doing on May 14?"

Leo tapped a key and glanced at his computer screen. "Looks clear. What's up?"

"I thought you might like to be my best man."

Now Luc had Leo's full attention. His older sibling, though still a couple inches shorter than Luc's six-three, was an imposing man. Built like a mountain, he looked more like a lumberjack than a numbers whiz.

He escaped the confines of his desk and cleared a front corner to lean on his hip and stare at his brother. "You're pulling my chain, right?"

"Why would you say that?"

"Three weeks ago I suggested you bring a date to Carole Ann's party, and you told me you weren't seeing anyone."

Luc shrugged. "Things happen."

Leo scowled, a black expression that had been known to make underlings quake in terror. "I can read you like a book. You're up to something. The last time I saw that exact look on your face, you were trying to convince Dad to let you take the Maserati for a weekend trip to Daytona."

"I have my own sports cars. I'm not trying to pull anything."

"You know what I mean." He changed tack. "Do I know her?"

Luc shrugged. "You've met."

"How long have *you* known her? It's not like you to go all misty-eyed over a one-night stand."

"I can assure you that I've known her for a very long time."

"But you've just now realized you're in love."

"A man doesn't have to be in love to want a woman."

"So it's lust."

"I think we've gotten off track. I asked if

you would be my best man. A simple yes or no will do."

"Damn it, Luc. Quit being so mysterious. Who is she? Will I get to see her anytime soon?"

"I haven't decided. We've been concentrating on each other. I don't want to spoil things. Just promise me you'll show up when and where I say on the fourteenth. In a tux."

The silence was deafening. Finally, Leo stood up and stretched. "I don't like the sound of this. When it all goes to hell, don't come crying to me. Your libido is a piss-poor businessman. Be smart, baby brother. Women are generally not worth the bother."

Luc understood his brother's caution. They had both been burned by love at a tender age, but thankfully had wised up pretty fast. What Leo didn't know, though, was that Luc had a plan. *Revenge* was a strong word for what he had in mind. He didn't hate Hattie Parker. Quite the contrary. All he wanted was for her to understand that while he might still find her sexually attractive, he was completely immune to any emotional connection. No hearts and flowers. No protestations of undying devotion.

He was no longer a kid yearning for a pretty girl. This time *he* had the power. *He* would be calling all the shots. Hattie needed him, and her vulnerability meant that Luc would have her in his house…in his bed…under his control. Perhaps *revenge was* too strong a word. But when all was said and done, Hattie Parker would be out of his system…for good.

Hattie was ready to scream. Moving anytime was a huge chore, but add a baby to the mix, and the process was darned near impossible. She'd finally gotten Deedee down for a nap and was wrapping breakables in the kitchen when her cell phone rang. She jerked it up and snarled, "What?"

The long silence at the other end was embarrassing.

"Sorry," she said, her throat tight with tears of frustration.

Luc's distinctive tones were laced with humor. "I don't think I've ever heard you lose your temper. I kind of like it."

"Don't be silly," she said, shoving a lock of

damp hair from her forehead. "What do you want?"

"Nothing in particular. I was checking in to see if you needed anything."

"A trio of muscular guys would be nice."

Another silence. "Kinky," he said, his voice amused but perhaps a tad hoarse.

Her face flamed, though he couldn't see her. "To help with moving," she muttered. "I wouldn't know what else to do with them. This mothering thing is hard work."

"Why, Hattie Parker. Are you hinting for help?"

"Maybe." Deedee was a good baby, but being a single parent was difficult. Hattie no longer felt as panicked as she had in the beginning. Much of the daily routine of dealing with an infant seemed easier now. But Deedee had been restless the three nights since Hattie had dined with Luc. Perhaps the baby was picking up on Hattie's unsettled emotions. And to make matters worse, Eddie had begun sending a harassing string of vague emails and texts. Clearly to keep Hattie on edge. And it was working.

Luc sighed audibly. "I would have hired a moving crew already, but you're always so damned independent, I thought you would pitch a fit and insist on doing it yourself."

"I've grown up, Luc. Some battles simply aren't worth fighting. I know when I'm in over my head."

"I'm sorry. I made a stupid assumption. It won't happen again."

The conversation lagged once more. She looked at the chaos in her kitchen and sighed. "Do you know yet when we're going to sit down and go over the finer points of our marriage agreement?"

"I thought perhaps tomorrow evening. When does Deedee go down for the night?"

"Usually by eight…if I'm lucky."

"What if I come over to your place then, so she won't have to be displaced. I'll bring food."

"That would be great."

"Have you heard any more from your brother-in-law?"

"Nothing specific." No need at the moment to involve Luc in Eddie's bluster. "He likes to throw his weight around. Right now, he's got the perfect setup. I'm babysitting for him, but when he's ready, he'll grab Deedee."

"I hope you don't mean that literally."

"He's not that stupid. At least, I don't think he is."

"Try not to worry, Hattie. Everything is going to fall into place."

For once, it seemed as if Luc was right. Deedee went to sleep the following evening without a whimper. Hattie found an unworn blouse in the back of her closet with the tags still attached. She'd snagged it from a clearance rack at Bloomingdale's last January, and the thin, silky fabric, a pale peach floral, was the perfect weight for a spring evening.

Paired with soft, well-worn jeans, the top made her look nice but casual…not like she was trying too hard to impress. Unfortunately, Luc showed up ten minutes early, and she was forced to open the door in her bare feet.

His eyes flashed with masculine appreciation when he saw her. "You don't look frazzled to me, Hattie."

She stepped back to let him in. "Thanks. Today was much calmer, maybe because the moving company you hired promised to be here first thing in the morning. And I was able to actually take a shower, because the baby took a two-hour morning nap."

As she closed the door, he surveyed her apartment. "No offense, but I don't see any point in storing most of this stuff. Let the movers take the bulk of it to charity, and bring only the things that are personal or sentimental with you."

She bit her lip. It had occurred to her that this subject would have to be broached, but she hadn't anticipated it would come so soon. "The thing is…"

"What are you trying to say?" He tossed the duffel bag he'd been carrying in a chair and deposited two cloth grocery bags in the kitchen. Then he turned to face her. "Is there a problem?"

She shifted from one foot to the other. Luc was wearing a suit and tie, and she felt like Daisy Duke facing off with Daddy Warbucks. "This union won't last forever. After all the money you're spending to help Deedee and me, you shouldn't have to finance the next phase of my life, as well. I thought it might be prudent to have something to fall back on in the future."

He nudged a corner of her navy plaid futon/chair with the toe of his highly polished wing tip, giving the sad, misshapen piece a dismissive glance. "When that happens, I won't cast off you and the child to live with cheap, secondhand furniture. I have a reputation to uphold in this town. Image is everything. You're going to have to face the truth, Hattie. You're marrying a rich man—whether you like it or not."

The mockery in his words and on his face was not veiled this time. He was lashing out at her for what she'd done in the past. Fair enough. Back then she had made a big deal about their stations in life. Luc's money gave him power, and Hattie had been taught at her mother's knee never to let a man have control.

The man Hattie called "daddy" was really her stepfather. As a nineteen-year-old, her mother had been that most naive of clichés...the secretary who had an affair with her boss. When Hattie's mom told her lover she was pregnant, he tossed her aside and never looked back.

Hattie lifted her chin. "It was never about the money," she insisted. "Or not *only* the money. Look at what your life has become, Luc. You're the CEO of a Fortune 500 company. I'm a public school teacher. I clip coupons and drive a ten-year-old car. Even before I began helping with my mother's finances, I lived a very simple lifestyle."

He curled a lip. "Is this where I cue the violins?"

"Oh, forget it," she huffed. "This is an old argument. What's the point?"

He shrugged. "What's the point indeed?" He picked up the duffel bag. "Dinner will keep a few minutes. Do you mind if I change clothes? I came straight from the office."

"The baby is asleep in my room, but the bathroom's all yours. I'll set out the food."

She had rummaged in the bags only long enough to see that Luc's largesse was nothing as common as pizza, when a loud knock sounded at the door. She glanced through the peephole and drew in a breath. Eddie. Good grief. Reluctantly, she opened the door.

He reeked of alcohol and swayed slightly on his feet. "Where's my baby girl? I want to see her."

She shushed him with a quick glance over her shoulder. "She's in bed. Babies sleep at this hour of night. Why don't you call me in the morning, and we'll agree on a time for you to come by?"

He stuck a foot in the doorway, effectively

keeping her from closing him out. "Or why don't I call the police and tell them you've kidnapped my kid?"

It was an idle threat. They both knew it. Hattie had already consulted a lawyer, and a nurse at the hospital had heard Angela's dying request. Nevertheless, Eddie's bluster curled Hattie's stomach. She didn't want to be in the middle of a fight with Deedee as the prize.

"Go away, Eddie," she said forcefully, her voice low. "This isn't a good time. We'll talk tomorrow."

Without warning, he grabbed her shoulders and manhandled her backward into the apartment. "Like hell." He shoved her so hard, she stumbled into the wall. Her head hit with a muffled thud, and she saw little yellow spots.

He lunged for her again, but before his meaty fists could make contact, Luc exploded down the hallway, grabbed the intruder by the neck and put a chokehold on him. Eddie's face turned an alarming shade of purple before Hattie could catch her breath.

Luc was steely-eyed. "Call the cops."

"But I don't want…"

His expression gentled. "It's the right thing to do. Don't worry. I'm not leaving you to deal with this alone."

The response to the 911 call was gratifying. Just before the two uniformed officers arrived, Luc stuck his face nose to nose with Eddie's. "If I ever see you near my fiancée again, I'll tear you apart. Got it?"

Eddie was drunk enough to be reckless. "Fiancée? Yeah, right. If she was telling my daddy the truth about you and her, then where's the fancy diamond ring?"

"I had to order it," Luc responded smoothly. "It happens to be in my pocket even as we speak. But some jackass has ruined our romantic evening."

The conversation ended abruptly as Hattie opened the door to the police. They took Luc's statement, handcuffed Eddie and were gone in under twenty minutes.

In the sudden silence, Hattie dropped into a chair, her legs boneless and weak in the aftermath of adrenaline. Thank God the baby hadn't been awakened by all the commotion.

Luc crouched beside her, his eyes filled with

concern. "Let me see your head." He parted her hair gently, exclaiming when he saw the goose egg that had popped up.

She moved restlessly. "I'm fine. Really. All I need is some Tylenol. And a good night's sleep."

Luc cursed under his breath. "Don't move." After bringing her medicine and water with which to wash down the tablets, he created a makeshift ice bag with a dish towel and pressed it to the side of her head. "Hold this." He lifted her in his arms and laid her gently on the ugly sofa. "Rest. I'll fix us a couple of plates."

He was back in no time. The smells alone made Hattie want to whimper with longing. Her stomach growled loudly.

He put a hand on her shoulder. "No need to get up yet. I'll feed you."

"Don't be ridiculous." But when she tried to sit upright, her skull pounded.

He eased her back down. "You don't have to fight me over every damn thing. Open your mouth." He fed her small manageable bites of chicken piccata and wild rice. While she chewed and swallowed, he dug into his own portion.

Hattie muttered in frustration when one of her

mouthfuls landed on the sofa cushion. "See what you made me do…"

"Don't worry," he deadpanned. "A few stains could only help this monstrosity."

She eyed him, openmouthed, and then they both burst into laughter. Hattie felt tears sting the backs of her eyes. She told herself it was nothing more than delayed reaction. But in truth, it was Luc. When he forgot to be on his guard with her, she saw a glimpse of the young man she had loved so desperately.

She wondered with no small measure of guilt if her long-ago defection had transformed the boy she once knew so well into the hard-edged, sardonic Luc. A million times over the years she had second-guessed her decision. It had been gratifying to establish a career and to stand on her own two feet. Her mother had been proud of Hattie's independence and success in her chosen field.

But at what cost?

When the last of the food was consumed, the mood grew awkward. Luc gathered their empty plates. "Stay where you are. You have to deal with Deedee in the morning, so you might as well rest while you can."

She lay there quietly, wondering bleakly how her life had unraveled so quickly. Two months ago she'd been an ordinary single woman with a circle of friends, a good job and a pleasant social life. Now she was a substitute parent facing a custody battle and trying to combat a tsunami of feelings for the man who had once upon a time been her other half, her soul mate. Was it any wonder she felt overwhelmed?

A trickle of water from melting ice slid down her cheek. She sat up and sucked in a breath when a hammer thudded inside her skull. The food she had eaten rolled unpleasantly in her stomach.

Luc frowned as he rejoined her, pausing only to take the wet dish towel and toss it on a kitchen counter. "We probably should make a trip to the E.R. to make sure you don't have a concussion."

"I'll be fine." She knew her voice lacked conviction, but it was hard to be stoic with the mother of all headaches.

Luc put his hands on his hips, his navy polo shirt stretching taut over broad shoulders and a hard chest. "I'll stay the night."

Four

Hattie gaped. "Oh, no. Not necessary."

"We have the baby to think of, too. You probably won't rest very well tonight, and you'll likely need an extra hand in the morning. I'll sleep on the couch. It may be ugly as sin, but it's long and fairly comfortable. I'll be fine."

Hattie was torn. Having Luc in her small apartment was unsettling, but the encounter with Eddie had shaken her emotionally as well as physically, and she was dead on her feet.

She shrugged, conceding defeat. "I'll get you towels and bedding." She brushed by him, inhaling for a brief instant the tang of citrusy aftershave and the scent of warm male.

When she returned moments later, he was on the phone with Ana, letting her know he wouldn't be home that evening. It touched her that he would be so considerate of people who were in his employ. He was a grown man. He had no obligation to let anyone know his schedule or his whereabouts.

But wasn't that what had drawn her to him in the beginning? His kindness and his humor? Sadly, his personality had an edge now, a remoteness that had not existed before.

She began making up the sofa, but he stopped her as soon as he hung up. "Go to bed, Hattie. I'm not a guest. I don't need you waiting on me. I can fend for myself."

She nodded stiffly. "Good night, then."

He lifted a shoulder, looking diffident for a moment. "May I see her?"

"The baby?" Well, duh. Who else could he mean?

"Yes."

"Of course."

He followed her down the short hallway into the bedroom. A small night-light illuminated the crib. Luc put his hands on the railing and stared down at the infant sleeping so peacefully. Hattie hung back. Her chest was tight with confused emotions. Had things gone differently in the past, this scene might have played out in reality.

A couple, she and Luc, putting their own daughter to bed before retiring for the night.

Luc reached out a hand, hovered briefly, then lightly stroked Deedee's hair. She never stirred. He spoke softly, his back still toward Hattie. "She doesn't deserve what has happened to her."

Hattie shook her head, eyes stinging. "No. She doesn't. I can't let Eddie take her. She's so innocent, so perfect."

Luc turned, his strong, masculine features shadowed in the half-light. His somber gaze met her wary one, some intangible link between them shrouding the moment in significance. "We'll keep her safe, Hattie. You have my word."

Quietly, he left the room.

Hattie changed into a gown and robe. Ordinarily, she slept in a T-shirt and panties, but with Luc in the house, she needed extra armor.

She folded the comforter and turned back the covers before heading for the bathroom. Well, shoot. She'd forgotten to give Luc even the basics.

Taking a new toothbrush from the cabinet, she returned to the living room. "Sorry. I meant to give you this. There's toothpaste on the counter, and if you want to shave in the morning—"

She stopped dead, her pulse jumping. Luc stood before her wearing nothing but a pair of gray knit boxers, which left little to the imagination. Every inch of his body was fit and tight. His skin was naturally olive-toned, and the dusting of fine black hair on his chest made her want to stroke it to see if it was as soft as she remembered.

Long muscular thighs led upward to... She gulped. As she watched in fascination, his erection grew and flexed. She literally couldn't move. Luc didn't seem at all embarrassed, despite the fact that her face was hot enough to fry an egg.

"Thank you for the toothbrush." A half smile lifted one corner of his mouth.

She extended the cellophane-wrapped package gingerly, making sure her fingers didn't touch his. "You're welcome."

And still she didn't leave. The years rolled away. She remembered with painful clarity what it was like to be held tightly to that magnificent chest, to feel those strong arms pull her close, to experience the hard evidence of his arousal thrusting against her abdomen.

His gaze was hooded, the line of his mouth now almost grim. "Like what you see?"

The mockery was deliberate, she had no doubt…as if to say *you were so foolish back then. Look what you gave up.*

Heat flooded her body. The robe stifled her. She wanted to tear it off, to fling herself at Luc. But her limbs couldn't move. She was paralyzed, caught between bitter memories of the past and the sure knowledge that Luc Cavallo was still the man who could make her soar with pleasure.

"Answer me, Hattie," he said roughly. "If you're going to look at me like that, I'm damn sure going to take the invitation."

Her lips parted. No sound came out.

The color on his cheekbones darkened and his eyes flared with heat. "Come here."

No soft preliminaries. No tentative approach.

Luc was confident, controlled. He touched only her face, sliding his hands beneath her hair and holding her still so his mouth could ravage hers. His tongue thrust between her lips—invading, dominant, taking and not giving. She was shaking all over, barely able to stand. He kissed her harder still, muttering something to himself she didn't quite catch.

She felt the push of his hips. Suddenly, her body came to life with painful tingles of heat. Her arms went around his waist, and she kissed him back. But when his fingers accidentally brushed the painful knot on her skull, she flinched.

Instantly, he cursed and thrust her away, his gaze a cross between anger and incredulity. "Damn you. Go to bed, Hattie."

If she had been a Victorian heroine, she might have swooned at this very moment. But she was made of sterner stuff. She marshaled her defenses, muttered a strangled good-night and fled.

Aeons later it seemed, she rolled over and flung an arm over her face. Bright sunshine peeked in through a crack between the curtains. She had slept like the dead, deeply, dreamlessly. A glance at the clock stopped her heart. It was nine o'clock. Deedee. Dear heaven. The baby was always up by six-thirty.

She leaped from the bed, almost taking a nose-dive when the covers tangled around her feet.

The crib was empty. She sucked in a panicked breath, and then her sleep-fuddled brain began to function.

Luc. Memories of his kiss tightened her nipples and made her thighs clench with longing. She touched her lips as the hot sting of tears made her blink and sniff. Ten years was a lifetime to wait for something that was at once so terrible and so wonderful.

She opened her bedroom door and simultaneously heard the sound of childish gurgles and smelled the heavenly aroma of frying bacon. Luc stood by the stove. Deedee was tucked safely in her high chair nearby.

He glanced up, his features impassive. "Good morning."

The baby squealed in delight and lurched toward Hattie. Luc unfastened the tray and handed her off. "I fed her a bottle and half a jar of peaches. I didn't want to give her anything else until I checked with you." The words were gruff, as if he'd had to force them from his throat.

Hattie cuddled the baby, stunned that Luc had taken over with such relaxed competence. Not that she didn't think he was capable. But she had never witnessed him with children, and she was shocked to see him so calm and in control, especially when Hattie herself had experienced a few rough moments in the last six weeks.

He started cracking eggs into a bowl. "This will be ready in five, and the movers will be showing up shortly. You might want to get dressed. I can handle Deedee."

Hattie held the baby close, realizing with chagrin that she had jumped out of bed and never actually donned her robe. The sheer fabric of her nightie revealed far too much. "She'll be fine with me." Suddenly she noticed the sheaf of legal papers on the nearby coffee table. "Luc... I'm so sorry. With everything that happened, we never did get around to dealing with the marriage stuff."

He popped two slices of bread into her toaster. "No worries. We'll have time later today."

She hesitated, eager to leave the room, but feeling oddly abashed that he had watched her sleeping...without her knowledge. Though they had made love many times when they were together, only once or twice had they enjoyed the luxury of spending the night together.

She cleared her throat. "Thank you for getting up with the baby. I can't believe I didn't hear her."

He shrugged. "I'm an early riser. I enjoyed spending time with her. She's a charming child."

"You haven't seen her throw a temper tantrum yet," she joked. "Batten down the hatches. She has a great set of lungs."

He paused his efficient preparations, the spatula in midair. "You're doing a great job. She's lucky to have you as her mother." His eyes and his voice were serious.

"Thanks." Despite the task he had undertaken, nothing about the setting made Luc look at all domestic: quite the opposite. Luc Cavallo was the kind of man you'd want by your side during a forced jungle march. He possessed a self-confidence that was absolute.

But that resolute belief in his own ability to direct the universe to his liking made Hattie uneasy. In asking for his help, she had unwittingly given him the very power she had refused to allow in their previous relationship. Even if she had second thoughts now, the situation was already beyond her control.

* * *

The contents of the small apartment were packed, boxes loaded and rooms emptied by 12:30. Luc had already paid out the remainder of Hattie's lease. All that was left for her to do was turn in her keys to the super and follow Luc out to the car where Sherman was waiting. But there she balked. "I'll follow you in my car."

Luc frowned. "I thought we had this discussion."

"I like my car. I'm sentimentally attached to my car. I'm not giving it away."

The standoff lasted only a few seconds. Luc shrugged, his expression resigned. "I'll see you at the house."

It was a small victory, but it made Hattie feel better. Luc had a habit of taking charge in ways that ostensibly made perfect sense, but left Hattie feeling like a helpless damsel in distress. She had *asked* for his help, but that didn't mean she'd let him walk all over her.

She strapped Deedee into the old, shabby car seat and slid into the front, turning the key in the ignition and praying the car would start. That would be the final indignity.

As their little caravan pulled away from the

curb, Hattie glanced in the rearview mirror for one last look at her old life slipping away. Her emotions were not easy to define. Relief. Sadness. Anticipation. Had she sold her soul to the devil? Only time would tell.

Luc experienced a sharp but distinct jolt of satisfaction when Hattie stepped over his threshold. Something primitive in him exulted. She was coming to him of her own free will. She'd be under his roof...wearing his ring. Ten years ago he'd let his pride keep him from trying to get her back. That, and his misguided belief that he had to respect her wishes. But everything was different this time around. *He* was calling the shots.

The attraction was still there. He felt it, and he knew she did, as well. Soon she would turn to him out of sheer gratitude, or unfulfilled desire or loneliness. And then she would be his. He'd waited a long time for this. And no one could fault him. He was giving Hattie and her baby a home and security.

If he extracted his pound of flesh in the process, it was only fair. She owed him that much.

He left them to get settled in, with Sherman and

Ana hovering eagerly. After changing clothes, he drove to the office and threw himself into the pile of work that had accumulated during his unaccustomed morning off.

But for once, his concentration was shot. He found himself wishing he was back at the house, watching Hattie…playing with the baby…anticipating the night to come.

He called home on the drive back. It wasn't late, only six-thirty. Hattie answered her cell.

"Hello, Luc."

He returned the greeting and said, "Ana has offered to look after Deedee this evening. I thought we might go out for a quiet dinner and discuss business."

Business? He winced. Did he really mean to sound so cavalier?

Hattie's response was cool. "I don't want to take advantage of Ana's good nature."

"You're not, I swear. It was her idea. Little Deedee has a way of making people fall in love with her. I'll be there to pick you up in twenty minutes."

It was only dinner. With a woman who had already rejected him once. Why was his heart beating faster?

* * *

Unfortunately for Hattie, the black dress had to do duty again. This time she had no inclination to wear Luc's necklace. Not for a *business* dinner. She tied a narrow tangerine scarf around her neck and inserted plain gold hoops in her ears.

She was ready and waiting in the foyer when he walked in the front door.

Luc seemed disappointed. "Where's the baby?"

Hattie grimaced, her nerves jumping. "She's taking an early evening nap. I couldn't get her to sleep much at all this afternoon...the uncertainty of a new place, I think. She was cranky and exhausted."

"Too bad. Well, in that case, I guess we can get going."

The restaurant was lovely—very elegant, and yet not so pretentious that Hattie felt uncomfortable. The sommelier chatted briefly with Luc and then produced a zinfandel that met with Luc's approval.

Hattie was persuaded to try a glass. "It's really good," she said. "Fruity but not too sweet."

He leaned back in his chair. "I thought you'd like it."

They enjoyed a quiet dinner, sticking to innocuous topics, and then afterward, Luc reached into a slim leather folder and extracted a sheaf of papers. "My lawyers have drawn up all the necessary documents. If you wish, you're welcome to have a third-party lawyer go over them with you. I know from experience that legalese is hard to wade through at times."

She took the documents and eyed them cautiously. "I have someone who has been helping me with the custody issues," she said, already skimming the lines of print. "I'll get her to take a look." Most of it was self-explanatory. When she reached page three of the prenup, her eyebrows raised. "It says here that if and when the marriage dissolves, I'll be entitled to a lump sum payment of $500,000."

He drummed the fingers of one hand on the table. His skin was dark against the snowy-white cloth. "You don't think that's fair?"

"I think it's outrageous. You don't owe me anything. You're doing me a huge favor. I don't plan to walk away with half a million dollars. Put something aside for Deedee's education if you want to, but we need to strike that line."

His jaw tightened. "The line stays. That's a deal breaker."

She studied his face, puzzled and upset. "I don't understand."

He scowled at her, his posture combative. "You've thrown my wealth in my face the entire time I've known you, Hattie. And now you're using it to protect someone you love. I don't have a problem with that. But I'll be damned when that day comes if I'll let anyone say I threw you out on the street destitute."

Her lip trembled, and she bit down on it…hard. Luc was a proud man. Perhaps until now she had never really understood just how proud he was. She was sure his heart had healed after she broke up with him. But maybe the dent to his pride was not so easily repaired.

She owed him a sign of faith. It was the least she could do after treating him so shabbily in the past. He was an honorable man. That much hadn't changed. She reached into her purse for a pen and turned to the first yellow sticky tab. With a flourish, she signed her name.

He put a hand over hers. "Are you sure you don't want someone to look over this with you?"

She shivered inwardly at his touch. "I'm sure," she said, her words ragged.

He released her and watched intently as she signed one page after another. When it was all done, she handed the documents back to him. "Is that it?"

Luc tucked the paperwork away. "I have a couple of other things I think we need to discuss, but it requires a private setting. We'll be more comfortable at home."

"Oh." Her scintillating response didn't faze him. He seemed perfectly calm. He summoned their waiter, paid the check and stood to pull out her chair. As they exited the restaurant, she was hyperaware of his warm hand resting in the small of her back.

Hattie was silent on the drive back. Her skin was hot, her stomach pitchy. What on earth could he mean? Sex? It seemed the obvious topic, but she had assumed they might work up to that gradually…after they were married. She hadn't anticipated talking about it so bluntly or openly. They had been as close as two people could be once upon a time. But that was long, long ago.

Was she willing to go to his bed? To be his wife

in every sense of the word? He was well within his rights as a husband to insist.

Did she expect him to be faithful in the context of a sham marriage? And if Luc no longer wanted to be intimate with Hattie, was it fair to deny him physical satisfaction?

She wouldn't lie to herself. She wanted Luc.

Dear Lord, what was she going to say?

In a cowardly play for more time, she stalled when they got back to the house. "I'd like to check on the baby and change clothes. Is that okay? It won't take me long."

Luc dropped his keys into the exquisite Baccarat dish on the table in the foyer. "Take your time. I'll meet you in the den when you're ready."

Five

Wearing ancient jeans and a faded Emory T-shirt, Luc sprawled on the leather sofa and stared moodily at the blank television screen. Was he insane? *Power.* A nice fantasy. Clearly he was fooling himself. What man was ever really in control when his brain ceded authority to a less rational part of his body?

Just being close to Hattie these last few days had caused him to resort to cold showers. He told himself that his physical response to her was nothing more than a knee-jerk reaction to memories…to sensual images of the way he and Hattie had burned up the sheets.

She'd been a virgin when they met, a shy, reserved girl with big eyes and a wary take on the world. As if she was never quite sure someone wasn't going to pull the rug out from under her feet.

He'd been embarrassed to tell her how many girls he'd been with before meeting her. A horny teenager with unlimited money at his disposal was a dangerous combination. In high school, he'd been too concerned about keeping his body in shape for sports to dabble in drugs. And even drinking, a rite of passage for adolescent boys, didn't hold much allure. Perhaps because he had grown up in a house where alcohol was freely available and handled wisely.

But sex…hell, he'd had a lot of sex. Money equals power…even sixteen-year-old girls could figure that out. So Luc was never without female companionship, unless he chose to hang with his buddies.

When Hattie came into his life, everything changed. She was different. She liked him, but his money didn't interest her. At first, he thought her attitude might be a ploy to snag his attention. But as they got to know each other, he realized that she really didn't give a damn that he was loaded.

She expected thoughtfulness from him, attention to her likes and dislikes. She wanted him to *know* her. And that was something money couldn't buy.

It was only much, much later that he realized his money was actually a stumbling block.

A faint noise made him turn his head. Hattie hovered in the doorway, her sun-streaked blond hair pulled back into a short ponytail, her feet bare. She was dressed as casually as he was.

He patted the seat beside him. "Would you like more wine?" The upcoming conversation might flow more easily if she relaxed.

She shook her head as she perched gingerly on the far end of the couch, tucking her legs beneath her. "No, thanks. Water would be nice." Her toenails were painted pale pink. The sight of them did odd things to his gut.

He went to the fridge behind the bar, extracted two Perriers and handed her one. As he sat back down, he allowed the careful distance she had created to remain between them. It meant she was nervous, and that gave him an edge. He handed her a slim white envelope. "We'll start with this." Inside were three credit cards with her soon-to-be name, Hattie Parker Cavallo, already imprinted.

She extracted them with patent reluctance. "What are these?"

He stretched an arm along the back of the sofa. "As my wife, you'll need a large wardrobe. I entertain frequently, and I also travel often. When it's feasible, I'd like you and Deedee to accompany me. In addition, I want you to outfit the nursery upstairs. I've put a selection of baby furniture catalogs in the desk drawer in your bedroom. Ana will show you the suite I picked out for Deedee. If it doesn't meet with your approval, we'll decide on another."

She paled, her eyes dark and haunted.

He ground his teeth. "What's wrong?"

She shrugged helplessly. "I…I feel like you're taking over my life. Like I've lost all control."

His fists clenched instinctively, and he had to force himself to relax. "I understood there was some sense of urgency to the situation…that we needed to back up your lie quickly."

"There is…and we do…but…"

"But what? Do you disagree with any of the arrangements I've made thus far?"

"No, of course not."

"Then I don't understand the problem."

She jumped to her feet and paced. With her back to him, he could see the way the soft, worn jeans cupped her butt. It was a very nice butt. With an effort, he dragged his attention back to the current crisis.

She whirled to face him. "I'm used to taking care of myself." The words were almost a shout.

Something inside him went still...crouched like a tiger in waiting. He feigned a disinterest he didn't feel. "We don't have to get married at all, Hattie. My team of lawyers loves going for the kill. Custody situations aren't their usual fare, but with Eddie in self-destruct mode, it shouldn't be too hard to convince a judge that you're the obvious choice to raise Deedee." He paused, risking everything on a gamble, a single toss of the dice. "Is that what you want?"

Hattie pressed two fingers to the center of the forehead, clearly in pain. Her entire body language projected misery. "I want my sister back," she said…and as he watched, tears spilled down her wan cheeks.

He tried to leave her alone, he really did. But her heartbreak twisted something inside his chest. She didn't protest when he took her in his arms, when he pulled the elastic band from her ponytail and stroked her hair, careful not to further hurt her injury.

She felt fragile in his embrace, but he knew better. Her backbone was steel, her moral compass a straight arrow.

The quiet sobs didn't last long. He felt and sensed the moment she pulled herself together. She stiffened in his embrace. Though it went against his every inclination, he released her and returned to his seat on the sofa. He took a swig of sparkling water and waited her out.

She studied a painting on the wall. It was a Vermeer he'd picked up at an auction in New York last year. The obscure work immortalized a young woman in her tiny boudoir as she bent at the waist to fasten her small shoe. The play of light on the girl's graceful frame fascinated Luc. He'd bought it on a whim, but it had quickly become one of his favorite pieces. Impulse drove him at times—witness the way he'd agreed so quickly to this sham marriage.

But in the end, his impulses usually served him well.

He grew impatient. "I asked you a question, Hattie. Do you want this marriage? Tell me."

She turned at last, her fists clenched at her sides. "If I don't go through with this, Eddie's family will know I lied. And they'll use it against me. I don't have a choice."

Her fatalistic attitude nicked his pride. His heart hardened, words tumbling out like cold stones. "Then we'll do this my way. You can't run out on me this time, Hattie. I love irony, don't you?"

His sarcasm scraped her nerves. She was being so unfair. Luc had done everything she had asked of him and more. He didn't deserve her angst and criticism. She owed him more than she could ever calculate.

The fact that her body still ached for his only complicated matters.

Swallowing her aversion to the feeling that she was being bought and paid for, she sat back down and summoned a faint smile. "Giving a woman that much plastic is dangerous. Should we discuss a budget?"

His expression was inscrutable. "I know you pretty well, Hattie Parker. I doubt seriously if you'll bankrupt me." He reached in his pocket and pulled out a small velvet box, laying it on the cushion between them. "This is next on the agenda. I thought it was customary to make such things a surprise, but given your current mood, perhaps I should return it and let you choose your own."

She picked up the box and flipped back the lid. *This* was a flawless diamond solitaire. Clearly he understood her style, because the setting was simple in the extreme. But the rectangular stone that flashed and sparkled was easily four carats.

She bit her lip. "It's lovely," she said, squeezing the words from a tight throat. He made no attempt to take her hand and do the honors. She told herself she was glad. When she slid the ring onto her left hand, the brilliant stone seemed to take on a life of its own.

"So you don't want to exchange it? I wouldn't want to be accused of controlling your life."

His tone was bland, but she felt shame, never-theless. "I love it, Luc. Thank you."

It was his turn to get up and pace. "I've made some preliminary wedding inquiries. Do you need or want a church wedding?"

Disappointment made her stomach leaden. Like most girls she had dreamed of her wedding day. "No. That's not necessary."

"Our family owns a small private island off the coast, near Savannah. If you're agreeable, we can have the ceremony there. The location precludes the possibility of Eddie or any of his relatives showing up to make a scene. Do you have someone you'd like to stand up with you?"

She picked at a stray thread on the knee of her jeans, her mind in a whirl of conflicting thoughts. "My best friend, Jodi, would have been my choice, but her husband is in the military, and they were transferred to Japan two months ago. With Angela gone, well, I…"

"I'm sure Ana would be honored to help us out."

It was a good choice, and a logical one given the circumstances. "I'll ask her tomorrow."

"A honeymoon will be important," he said,

bending to turn on the gas logs in the fireplace. The spring evening had turned cool and damp.

"I'm not sure what you mean."

He turned to face her, his expression blank. "We can't risk any accusation that our marriage isn't real. I know you'll protest, but I really think we should go away for at least a week. Ana's niece is a college student working on her early childhood certification. I've already spoken to her, and she's willing to stay here at the house with Ana and Sherman while we're gone, to help with the baby."

Hattie gnawed her bottom lip. He'd neatly cut the ground from beneath her feet. Every argument anticipated and countered. It all made perfect sense. And it scared the heck out of her. "You seem to have thought of everything."

He shrugged. "It's what I do. As far as the wedding dress and the ceremony itself, I'll leave that to you. I have a good friend who is a justice of the peace. He's prepared to fly down with us and officiate."

"Who's going to be your best man?"

"Leo."

"Does he know about me...about Deedee?"

"I told him I was marrying someone he knew, but I left it at that. Leo will be there. But as far as he is concerned right now, this is a normal marriage. You and I will be the only people who will know the truth."

"You'd lie to your own brother?"

"I'll tell him the situation later…when it's a done deal."

"And your grandfather?"

"He's flying over for his big birthday party in the fall. I won't encourage him to come this time."

"I wonder if Leo will even remember me."

Luc chuckled. "My brother never forgets a beautiful woman. We'll get together with him for dinner when we come back from our honeymoon, and you can reminisce."

Hattie winced inwardly. Leo probably thought she was the worst kind of tease. Leading Luc on back in college and then dumping him. Leo would side with his brother, of course. Just one more thing to look forward to in her new, surreal life.

She took a deep breath. "When are we going to do this?"

"May 14 works for my schedule. I've cleared the week following for our honeymoon. Is there anywhere in particular you'd like to go? The company has a top-notch travel agent."

She smiled faintly. "Since I've never really *been* anywhere, I'll let you choose."

"I thought Key West might be nice…a luxurious villa on a quiet street. A private pool."

Her mouth dried. "Um, sure. Sounds lovely." Why did she suddenly have a vision of the two of them naked and…cavorting in the moonlight? *Dear heaven.* May 14 was two and a half weeks away. This was happening. This was real.

She couldn't wait any longer to address the elephant in the room. Or perhaps she was the only one who was worrying about it. Luc was a guy. Sex came as naturally to him as breathing. He probably thought nature would take its course.

But she needed to have things spelled out. "Luc?"

He rejoined her on the sofa, this time sitting so close to her that their hips nearly touched. Deliberately, he lifted her hand nearest him and linked their fingers. "What, Hattie? Permission to speak freely."

His light humor did nothing to alleviate her nerves. She squeezed his hand briefly and stood up again, unable to bear being so close to him when she was on edge. "I had a feeling earlier this evening…at dinner…that one of the things you wanted to discuss in private was sex. It makes sense…to talk about it, I mean. You're a virile man, and I assume you'll be faithful to our wedding vows. So no one can question the validity of our marriage. For the baby's sake."

His face darkened. "For the baby's sake…right. Because I assume that otherwise you could care less if I went to another woman for satisfaction."

He was angry, and she wasn't sure why. She picked up the elastic band he'd removed from her hair. With swift, jerky movements she put her ponytail back in place. She didn't want to think about how it felt to have his fingers combing through her hair, his hard, warm palms caressing her back.

"I'm trying to explain, Luc, that I'm okay with it."

"Okay with what?"

His black scowl terrified her. If she handled this wrong, he might back out entirely. "I understand that it makes sense for us to be intimate…while we're together. A man and a woman living in the same house…married. I'm willing.… That's all I wanted to say."

His lip curled. His dark eyes were impenetrable. "Well, you were right about one thing."

"I was?"

"I did want to talk about sex."

"I thought so."

"But while I am deeply touched by your desire to throw yourself on the sacrificial altar, I don't need your penance."

"I don't understand."

His legs were outstretched, propped on the coffee table. He feigned relaxation, but his entire body vibrated with intense emotion. "It's simple, Hattie. All I wanted to say was that it seems somewhat degrading to both of us to exchange *physical pleasure* for money."

The way he drawled the words *physical pleasure* made her belly tighten. "You're confusing me."

"Sex has nothing to do with this marriage agreement. Is that clear enough? If we end up in bed together, it will be because we both want it.

I'm attracted to you, Hattie…just as I would be to any beautiful woman. And I have a normal man's needs. I'll welcome you to my bed anytime. But you'll have to come to me. Your body is not on the bargaining table."

He was being deliberately cruel. Perhaps she deserved it. But humiliation swept through her in burning waves. She had offered herself up in all sincerity, and he had reduced the possibility of marital intimacy to scratching an itch.

Dimly, apprehensively, she began to understand what Luc was going to get out of this marriage. He was going to make her dance to his tune. He was going to make her beg.

And what scared her even more than being totally at his mercy was the inescapable knowledge that she would be the one to crack. And she might not make it through the honeymoon.

Six

The days before the wedding flew by. Hattie was consumed with setting up the nursery and shopping for an appropriate dress in which to become Mrs. Luc Cavallo.

After the embarrassing scene with Luc in the den, Hattie saw little of him. He spent four days in Milan at a conference, and when he returned to Atlanta, he worked long days, ostensibly getting caught up so he could be away for a week's vacation. No one at his office knew anything about a wedding.

Deedee was thriving. There had been no further word from Eddie, and on the surface, life seemed normal.... Or at least as normal as it could be given the current situation.

Sherman and Ana adored Deedee and spoiled her with toys and other gifts. Hattie relished being part of that circle. She had never known her own grandparents, and the new relationships she was building helped fill the emotional hole in her soul. Things might become awkward when the marriage ended, but she would worry about that when the time came.

The wedding was only four days away when trouble showed up. Not Eddie this time. A loud knock sounded at the front door midday, and Hattie answered it. Sherman was out back washing the cars, and Ana was making dinner preparations.

The man standing on the doorstep was familiar. "Leo," she said, her heart sinking. "Please come in."

"Well, isn't this nice," he sneered. "Playing lady of the manor, are we?"

She ignored his sarcasm. Clearly, he *did* remember her…and not fondly. "Luc's not home."

Leo folded his arms across his broad chest. "I came to see you." He was a physically intimidating man, and his brains more than equaled his brawn. Back in college he had played at flirting with her. Not seriously, just to get his brother's goat. But the look on his face at the moment said he'd just as soon toss her in the river as look at her.

"How did you know I was here?"

"I didn't. But I knew *something* was going on. My brother's been acting damn strangely. And now I know why."

Ana appeared, wiping her hands on a dish cloth. "Mr. Leo. How nice to see you." She turned to Hattie. "If you would like to step out back to the patio, I'd be happy to bring you a snack."

Leo smiled at the housekeeper, a warm, I'm-really-a-nice-guy smile. "Sounds wonderful, Ana. I've been running all day and missed lunch." He eyed Hattie blandly. "What a treat."

Hattie felt Leo's eyes boring into her back as they made their way through the house. She hadn't expected a warm welcome from Luc's brother, but she also hadn't anticipated this degree of antipathy from him. They sat down in wrought-iron chairs, and moments later Ana brought out a tray of oatmeal cookies and fresh coffee.

The older woman poured two cups and stepped

back. "I'll put the monitor in the kitchen, Hattie, so I'll be able to hear the baby if she wakes up."

Leo paled. As soon as the housekeeper was out of earshot, he swallowed half a cup of coffee and glared at Hattie over the rim of a bone china cup. His big hand dwarfed it. "Luc's a daddy?"

"No, of course not. Or not in the way you're thinking. Has he told you anything about my situation?" It was difficult to believe that Luc would cling to his intent of keeping Leo uninformed.

"Luc didn't tell me diddly squat. All he mentioned was that I should show up on the fourteenth wearing my tux when and where he said."

"Oh."

"Perhaps you'd like to fill me in." It wasn't a request.

"I'm sorry he's been keeping secrets from you. It's my fault." She quickly gave him the shortened version of the last two months. "I think that until the lawyers get a handle on this custody thing, Luc thinks the less said the better."

Leo ate two more cookies, eyeing her with a laserlike stare as he chewed slowly. "That's not why he didn't tell me. Luc knows I can keep my mouth shut. But he knew I would try to talk him out of this ridiculous sham of a marriage."

Hattie's heart sank. The two brothers were close. Could Leo, even now, derail what Luc and Hattie had set in motion?

She set down her cup so he wouldn't see her hand shaking. "Why would you do that? If you're worried about the money, or the company…you needn't be. I've already signed a prenup."

Leo snorted. "You may be a lot of things, Hattie, but even I know you're not a gold digger."

"Then why is this any of your business?" She heard the snap in her own voice and didn't care. What did Leo Cavallo have to gain by sticking his big Roman nose into her affairs?

He pulled his chair closer to the table, his knees almost touching hers beneath the glass. His accusatory mood made her want to run, but she refused to give him the satisfaction. He spoke softly, with menace. "Ten years ago, you almost destroyed my brother. You let him fall in love with you, encouraged it even. And then when he proposed, the first and only time he's ever done that by the way, you shut him down. A man has his pride, Hattie. You let things go too far. If you weren't going to love him back, why in the hell did you sleep with him? Why did you let him think you were his girl, his future?"

She bent her head, staring down at the crumbs on her plate. "That's just it, Leo. I did love him. I was sick with loving him."

"That's bull." He lifted her chin, his gaze boring into hers. "Women in love don't do what you did to Luc."

"That's not true," she cried. "We never would have worked out in the long term. I wasn't the right person to be his wife. I did the right thing by breaking it off. You know I did."

He let go of her and sat back, brooding, surly. "Then how do you explain this?" He waved a hand. "You damn sure appear to be enjoying the fancy house and the hired help."

"Don't be hateful."

"Not hateful, honey. Just stating the facts."

"This is all temporary."

"Does Luc know that?"

"Of course he does. When enough time has passed to make our marriage appear to be the real thing, we'll separate quietly. And I'll raise Deedee on my own."

"And what happens when my softhearted baby brother falls in love with the little girl sleeping upstairs? Will you tear his heart out again by taking her away?"

Hattie closed her eyes, regret raking her with sharp claws. "That won't happen," she said weakly.

"How do you know?" Leo asked quietly. "And how do you know he won't fall in love with *you* again?"

She laughed without amusement. "I can assure you *that* is not a possibility. Luc's helping me because he's a good man. But he's made it very clear that this is strictly business."

"And you believe him?"

"Why would he lie?"

"To protect himself perhaps?"

"From what?"

"The correct answer is *from whom*. You, Hattie. A man never forgets his first love. Why else would he turn his entire life upside down in a matter of days?"

"I think he's hoping for some payback, if you want to know the truth. I know I hurt him. I'm not stupid. This is his chance to be in control. To make me fall in line, not in love."

"How so?"

"He made it very clear that he has no feelings for me anymore."

Leo shook his head. "You don't know anything at all about men, sweetheart. If that's what he said, he's kidding himself. He sounds like a man who knows his own limits and is covering his ass."

Hattie mulled over Leo's words, torn between embarrassment and hope.

She was on the bed playing with Deedee when the master of the house came home. It surprised her that he sought her out. They had barely spoken a dozen words in the last week.

He looked tired. Not for the first time, she pondered the unfairness of what she had asked him to do. But what choice did she have? On her own, Eddie's family would have eaten her alive. And Luc had jumped at the opportunity to throw his weight around. So why did she feel guilty?

He sat down on the corner of the bed and grinned at Deedee. She wriggled her way across the mattress toward him in a sort of commando crawl. He scooped her up and held her toward the ceiling. "Hey, kiddo. What mischief have you been up to today?"

Deedee squealed with laughter, her round cheeks pink with exertion. Luc nuzzled her tummy and lowered her to blow raspberries against her belly button.

Hattie watched them, her heart warmed by the budding connection man and infant shared. "She really likes you."

Luc glanced at Hattie. "The feeling is mutual."

His obvious enjoyment of something as simple as playing with a baby brought Leo's words rushing back. In all the time Hattie had thought about what would happen when the marriage ended, she had never considered the toll on Luc and her niece. Deedee would still be young. She wouldn't even remember Luc after a few months. But would Luc grieve?

Damn Leo for planting doubts.

Luc let the baby loose to roam the mattress again. Hattie had surrounded the edge with pillows, so Deedee couldn't go far. When the child latched on to one of her favorite toys, Luc finally spoke directly to Hattie. "How was your day?"

The prosaic question surprised her somehow. She leaned back on her elbows. "They delivered the nursery furniture early this morning. Deedee has already napped twice in the new bed and pronounced it quite satisfactory."

"Good." Long awkward silence. "Are you ready for the weekend? Do you need anything?"

She sat up. "I'm pretty much packed. Ana has been helping me."

"And the dress?"

"I finally found what I wanted yesterday. I hope it will be appropriate."

"I'm sure it's fine."

Hattie sighed inwardly. Next thing you know, they'd be discussing the weather. She grabbed Deedee's ankle and pulled her toward the center of the bed. "Leo came by today."

That got Luc's attention. His eyes narrowed. "What did he want?"

"Well, apparently you neglected to mention that you were marrying me…or that I came with a baby. He wasn't happy."

Luc shrugged, his expression dangerous. "I

don't make decisions based on Leo's likes and dislikes. If he doesn't want to come to the wedding, Sherman can do the honors."

"Don't be so pigheaded. Leo loves you."

"Leo believes his fourteen-month head start gives him the obligation to run my life."

"I think you should call him."

Luc's face went blank, wiped clean of all emotion. "I'll see him soon enough."

"Fine. Be an arrogant jerk. See if I care."

Luc stood up, gazing down at Hattie with an odd expression. "Sherman and Ana have the night off."

"I know. Did you want me to fix you something for dinner?"

"I thought we could take the baby on a picnic."

"It's kind of late."

"It won't hurt her to stay up just this once. Will it?"

"I guess not. I'll need to change, though."

He eyed her snug yellow T-shirt and khaki shorts. "You're fine. Let's go. I'm starving."

Luc had a garage full of expensive cars for every occasion. They took one of the more sedate sedans, a sporty Cadillac, and Luc moved the car seat. On the way, he dialed his favorite Chinese restaurant for takeout. Ten minutes later a helpful employee ran three bags out to the curb. The young man smiled hugely when Luc handed over a hundred and told the kid to keep the change.

Hattie wasn't prepared for their destination. Atlanta had many lovely spots for al fresco dining, but Piedmont Park brought back too many memories. Had Luc chosen the location on purpose?

As Hattie freed Deedee from her seat, Luc gathered the food, a blanket from the trunk, a bottle of chilled wine and a corkscrew he'd added before they left the house. It was a perfect spring evening. The park was crowded, but after a few minutes' walk, they found a quiet spot away from Frisbees and footballs.

Deedee had eaten earlier, so Hattie buckled her into a small, portable seat with a tray and fed her Cheerios while Luc opened containers. The smells made Hattie's stomach growl.

She snagged an egg roll. "This looks heavenly. I'm probably going to make a pig of myself."

Luc ran his gaze from her long legs all the way up past her waist to her modest breasts. "A few extra pounds wouldn't do you any harm."

The intimacy in his voice caught her off guard. What kind of game was he playing?

They ate leisurely, rarely speaking, content to watch the action all around them. Hattie remembered their college days with wistfulness. Back then, Luc would already have had his head in her lap. She'd be stroking his hair, touching his chest.

She trembled inwardly as arousal made her weak with longing. Deedee was no help. Her little head slumped to the side as she succumbed to sleep. Hattie unbuckled her and lifted her free. Luc moved the seat, and together they tucked the baby between them.

Luc reclined on his side facing Hattie. "I heard from the lawyers today. They've spoken to their counterparts, and it seems that Eddie's trying to claim it was really your sister at the wheel that night. That he was confused by the impact and that was why he left the scene."

Hattie clenched her fists. "Please tell me that won't fly."

He propped up one knee. "The police report is pretty clear. But that doesn't mean the case won't drag on. I don't know what they're getting paid, but my guys said the other team doesn't seem to have trouble with Eddie committing perjury if it will get him off."

Hattie was stunned. Since when could a man literally murder other people by driving under the influence and not end up in prison?

Luc was attuned to her distress. He stroked the sleeping infant's back. "Try not to worry. I'm only keeping you informed. But I don't want you to obsess about this. Our bottom line is keeping Eddie away from Deedee. Some judges side with a biological parent automatically, but if it comes to a hearing—and it may not—we'll show proof that Eddie would be a danger to his own child."

Hattie shivered. "I hope you're right. Judges can be bought."

Luc's grin was feral. "Good thing I have deep pockets."

Moments later he surprised the heck out of her by falling asleep. As Hattie looked at man and baby, she realized an unpalatable truth. It would be dangerously easy to fall in love with Luc Cavallo again. The few men she had dated seriously in the last decade were shadows when held up against Luc's vibrant personality.

Hesitantly, she reached out and barely touched his hair. It was soft and thick and springy with the waviness he hated. Usually, he kept his cut conservatively short, but perhaps he'd been too busy for his customary barber visit, because she could see the beginnings of a curl at the back of his ear.

Something hot and urgent twisted in her belly. She wanted to lie down beside him, whisper in his ear, pull him on top of her and feel his powerful body mate with hers. Her hand shook as she pulled it back. She would go to him eventually. It was inevitable. And he would have the satisfaction of knowing that she had made a mistake in leaving him. He would taste her regret and know the scales had been evened.

Luc held all the power. She was helpless to stem the tide of the burgeoning desire she felt. It had only been lying dormant, waiting to be resurrected.

And no matter how much pain she would have to endure when the marriage ended, she would not be able to walk away from the temptation to once again be Luc Cavallo's lover.

Seven

The morning of May 14 dawned bright and clear. The entire household was up at first light. Ana brought Hattie breakfast in bed, toast and jam and half a grapefruit.

Hattie, who had been awake for some time, sat up, shoving the hair from her eyes. "You didn't have to do this."

Ana sat down on the edge of the bed. "A bride deserves special treatment on her wedding day. Sherman and Mr. Leo have taken Deedee outside for a walk in the stroller. All you need to do is relax and let the rest of us pamper you."

Hattie took a bite of toast and had trouble swallowing. Even the freshly brewed hot tea didn't help. Fear choked her. Panic hovered just off-stage. She wiped her hands on a soft damask napkin and looked at Ana. "Am I doing the right thing?"

A few nights ago, Luc and Hattie had decided the older couple needed to know the truth. Luc had hired round-the-clock security to be in place during the honeymoon, but it wasn't fair to leave Deedee's caregivers out of the loop.

Ana smoothed the embroidered bedspread absently. "Did I tell you that Mr. Luc offered Sherman and me an embarrassing amount of money if we wanted to retire?"

It seemed an odd answer to Hattie's question.

"I knew he gave you the option. But he told me you loved the house and didn't want to leave."

"As it was, he almost doubled our salaries. We're taking our first cruise this fall, nothing too fancy, but it will be a change of pace."

"Sounds like fun."

"The thing is, Hattie, I've worked my whole life. I wouldn't know what to do if I had to sit around all day. The previous owners of this grand old property were both in their nineties when they passed. They never had a family, and Sherman and I weren't able to have children, either. This is a big, wonderful house with all kinds of interesting history. But until you and Deedee moved in, it was missing something." She paused and smiled softly. "Mr. Luc wants to help you and that precious baby. What could be wrong with that?"

"But it isn't a real marriage. We're not a family."

Ana shrugged. "That may be true at the moment, but things happen for a reason. I've seen it too many times in my life not to believe that. Take it a day at a time. You'll be fine, Hattie dear. Now eat your breakfast and get in the shower. Mr. Luc's not one for running late."

Luc had chartered a private plane, and at ten-thirty sharp, it was wheels up. The short flight from Atlanta to the southeast coast of the state was a source of constant fascination for Deedee. She sat with Ana and Sherman, stuck her nose to the window and was uncustomarily still as she watched the clouds drift by.

Leo and Luc huddled together in the front row talking business and who knows what else. Luc's friend, who was to do the ceremony, sat with them. Hattie was left to chat with Ana's niece, Patti. The young woman's eyes were almost as big as Deedee's.

She took a Coke from the flight attendant and turned to Hattie with a grin. "I've never been on a plane before, and especially not one like this. I could get used to the lifestyle. Did you know the bathroom has *real* hand towels...not paper?"

Hattie smiled at the girl's enthusiasm. "I can't thank you enough for helping out while we're gone on our honeymoon."

Patti wrinkled her nose. "Well, I love kids, and when Mr. Cavallo offered to pay my fall tuition in exchange for the week, I wasn't about to say no. My aunt and uncle and I will take such good care of Deedee. You won't have to worry about a thing."

Hattie gulped inwardly. Her debts to Luc were piling up more quickly than she could calculate.

Before Hattie could catch her breath and gird herself for what was to come, the plane landed smoothly on a small strip of tarmac. Three large SUVs sat waiting for the wedding party. Once in the cars, they were all whisked away to a nearby dock where they boarded a sleek black cabin cruiser.

At first, Luc's island was nothing more than a speck against the horizon, but as the boat cut through the choppy waves, land came into view. Down at the water's edge, a large wooden pier had been festooned with white ribbons. Uniformed staff secured a metal ramp and soon everyone stood on dry land.

Hattie looked around with wonder. They were too far north in latitude for the island to have a tropical flavor, but it was enchanting in other ways. Ancient trees graced the windswept contours of the land, and birds of every color and size nested in limbs overhead and left dainty footprints in the wet sand.

Luc appeared at her side. "What do you think?"

She smiled up at him. "It's amazing...so peaceful. I love it, Luc. It's perfect."

"We're trying to get the state to designate it as a wildlife refuge. Leo and I have no plans to develop this place. But one day, when we're gone, we want it to be protected." He took her arm. "Let's go. There's more to see."

Hattie's skin tingled where he touched her.

Their hands were linked...perhaps he didn't notice. But the intimacy, intentional or not, was poignant to Hattie.

Dune buggies took the group up and over a crest to the far side of the island where a weathered but genteel guesthouse stood, built to blend into the landscape.

Luc helped her out of the fiberglass vehicle. "There's plenty of room inside for everyone to change. Will thirty minutes give you long enough? There's no real rush." He paused, and stared down at her, his expression pensive. "This is your day, Hattie. I know the circumstances aren't ideal, but you're doing a wonderful thing for Deedee."

For one brief moment, wistfulness crushed her chest as she wondered what it would have been like to marry Luc when she was twenty-one. Determinedly, she thrust aside regret. This was not the same situation at all. She lifted a hand and cupped his cheek. "Thank you, Luc. I don't know what I would have done if you had turned me away."

The space around them was ionized suddenly, the hot, sticky air heavy with unspoken emotions. She went up on her tiptoes and found his mouth with hers. Someone groaned. Maybe both of them. He tasted like all her memories combined, hot and sweet and dangerous.

But they were not alone.

Luc took a step backward, and her hand fell away. Something akin to pain flashed across his face. "We both want what's best for the baby," he said, his voice gruff. "That's the important thing."

Sherman and Patti tended to Deedee while Ana helped Hattie get dressed. Hattie disappeared into a well-appointed bathroom to freshen up and slip into an ivory bustier and matching silk panties. Ana stepped in briefly to help with buttons and then tactfully left Hattie alone.

The day was warm and humid, and Hattie was glad she had decided to wear her hair up. She tweaked the lace trim at her breasts, adjusted the deliberately casual knot of hair at the back of her head and looked into the mirror. Too bad Luc wouldn't get a chance to see her in the delicate garments. They made her feel feminine and desirable, and she had charged them to one of the new credit cards without a qualm.

Ana waited in the bedroom, the wedding dress draped over her arms. In a small exclusive boutique in Buckhead, Hattie had found exactly what she wanted. The off-white dress was made of watered silk fabric and chiffon. The halter neckline flattered her bust and the fitted drop waist fluffed out into several filmy layers that ended in handkerchief points. The ecru kid slippers she'd bought to match were trimmed in satin ribbons that laced at her ankles.

Both women blinked away tears when Ana zipped up the dress and turned Hattie to face the mirror. It was fairy-tale perfect for a beach wedding—definitely bridal, but spritely and whimsical. Truth be told, it was not really a "Hattie" sort of dress. But it was her wedding day, damn it, and she wanted to be beautiful for Luc.

Ana picked up the narrow tiara and pinned it carefully to the top of Hattie's head. It was the appropriate finishing touch.

The older woman fluffed the skirt and stepped back. "You look like an angel." Her expression sobered. "I'm so sorry your mother and sister aren't here with you."

Hattie hiccupped a sob. "Me, too."

Ana looked alarmed. "No crying, for heaven's sake. My fault. Shouldn't have said anything. Let's touch up your makeup and get outside. I'll bet good money you have an eager groom waiting for you."

Ana left to take her place, and for a moment, Hattie was alone with her thoughts. She couldn't say in all honesty that she had no doubts. But perhaps a lot of brides felt this way. Scared and hopeful.

There was a brief knock at the door. When Hattie opened it, Leo's large frame took up the entrance. He looked her over, head to toe. A tiny smile lifted a corner of his mouth. "You'll do, Parker." He handed her a beautiful bouquet of lilies and eucalyptus. "These are from my brother. He's impatient."

He held out his arm, and she put her hand on it, her palm damp. "I care about him, Leo…a lot."

"I know you do…which is the only reason I'm here. But God help me, Hattie…if you hurt him again, I'll make you pay."

Not exactly auspicious words to start a new life.

Leo escorted her to the corner of the house, just out of sight of the water's edge where the ceremony would take place. He bent and kissed her cheek, then stepped back. Perhaps he saw the sheer panic in her eyes, because he smiled again, a real smile this time. "Break a leg, princess." And then he was gone.

Hattie's cue was to be the opening notes of "Pachelbel's Canon." A sturdy boardwalk led from the porch of the house out over a small dune to the temporary platform and the wooden latticed archway where she and Luc would stand.

The music started. She clenched her fists and then deliberately relaxed them. One huge breath. Several small prayers. One foot in front of the other.

Afterward, she could not remember the exact details of her solitary journey to the altar. In keeping with the unorthodox nature of the marriage and the ceremony, she had decided to walk to Luc on her own. This was her decision, her gamble.

When she first caught sight of the groom, her breath lodged in her throat and she stumbled slightly. Though there were three other people framed against the vibrant blue-green of the ocean, she only had eyes for Luc. He was wearing a black tux…a formal morning coat and tails over a crisp white shirt and a gray vest.

His gaze locked on hers and stayed there as she traversed the final fifty feet. As she stepped beneath the arch and took her place by his side, she saw something hot and predatory flash in his dark eyes before he turned to face the justice of the peace.

Without looking at Hattie again, Luc reached out and took her right hand, squeezing it tightly. The officiant smiled at both of them. "We are gathered here today to witness the union of Luc Cavallo and Hattie Parker. Marriage is a…"

Hattie tried to listen…she really did. But her thoughts scattered in a million directions. Too many stimuli. The feel of Luc's hard, warm fingers twined with hers. The familiar tang of his aftershave, mingling with the scent of her bouquet. The muted roar of the nearby surf as waves tumbled onto shore.

If she had the power, she would freeze this moment. To take out later in the quiet of her bedroom and savor everything she missed the first time around.

Out of the corner of her eye, she could see the giant live oaks that cast shade and respite on this hot, windy day. Sherman and Patti stood guard over the stroller, which was draped in mosquito netting. Apparently, Deedee had decided to co-operate and sleep through it all.

Closer to hand, Ana smiled, her cheeks damp. She was wearing a moss-green designer suit that flattered her stocky frame and shaved ten years off her age. Hattie had no doubt that Luc had financed the expensive wedding finery.

For a split second Hattie caught Leo's eye. The resemblance between the two brothers was striking, but where Luc was classically hand-some, quieter and more reserved, Leo was larger than life. He winked at her deliberately, and she blushed, turning her attention back to the words that would make her Luc's wife.

"May I have the rings?"

Ana commandeered the bouquet, Hattie and Leo complied, and moments later, Hattie slid a plain gold band onto Luc's left hand. He returned the favor, placing a narrow circlet of platinum beside the beautiful engagement ring to which Hattie had yet to grow accustomed.

More words, a pronouncement and then the moment she had unconsciously been waiting for. "You may kiss the bride."

In unison, she and Luc turned. The breeze ruffled his hair. His expression was solemn, though his eyes danced. He took Hattie's hands in his. Time stood still.

Ten years…ten long years since she had been free to kiss him whenever she wanted.

He bent his head. His mouth brushed hers, lingered, pressed more insistently. His tongue coaxed. His arms tightened around her as her skirt tangled capriciously with his pant legs.

Her heart lodged in her throat, tears stung her eyes, and she moved her mouth against his.

Aeons later it seemed, a chorus of unison laughter broke them apart. Luc appeared as dazed as Hattie felt.

Suddenly, hugs and congratulations separated them, but every moment, Luc's eyes followed her.

They led their small parade back to the house. Hattie had only seen one of the bedrooms, but now they all entered the great room on the opposite side of the building. The ambience was rustic but elegant. Exposed beams of warmly-hued wood were strung with tiny white lights. Dozens of blush-pink roses in crystal vases decorated every available surface.

A single table covered in pale pink linen was set with exquisite china, crystal and silver. When they were all seated, with Luc and Hattie at the head, Leo stood up.

As a waiter deftly poured champagne for everyone, Leo raised his glass. "Luc here, my baby brother, is and will always be my best friend. When Mom and Dad drowned, out on that damned boat they loved so much, Luc and I were shipped off to Italy to live for three years with a grandfather we barely knew. The language was strange, we were a mess, but we had each other."

He paused, and Hattie saw the muscles in his throat work with emotion. He moved to stand between and behind the bride and groom, laying a hand on each of their shoulders. "To Luc and his beautiful bride. May they always be as happy as they are today."

Applause and cheers filled the room, and moments later, the unobtrusive waitstaff began serving lunch.

Hattie knew the food was delicious. And wine flowed like water. But she couldn't taste any of it.

She was married to Luc. For some undefined period of time in order to protect the baby she had grown to love. But at what price?

When Luc put his arm around her bare shoulders, her heartbeat wobbled and sped up. He leaned over to whisper in her ear. "Are you doing okay, Mrs. Cavallo?" Gently, he tucked a wayward wisp of her hair into place.

She nodded mutely.

Luc laughed beneath his breath. "It might help if you quit looking like a scared rabbit."

She shrugged helplessly. "I'm in over my head," she admitted quietly. "What have we done, Luc?"

He stroked her back as he answered a cheerful question from across the table. "Forget reality," he murmured. "Pretend we're on Fantasy Island. Maybe this is all a dream."

Beneath the table, his hand played with hers.

The silly, childish game restored her equilibrium. Moments later their intimate circle was broken as Deedee demanded, in a loud string of nonsense syllables, to be recognized.

Luc chuckled as he stood to take the baby from Sherman and handed her to Hattie. Immediately, Deedee reached for the tiara. She yanked on it before Luc could stop her, and soon Hattie's hair was askew.

Amidst shrieks of infant temper, the tiara was rescued, the baby given one of her toys and the two at the head table became three. Luc tickled one chubby thigh, making Deedee chortle with laughter. He growled at her playfully and reached to take her in his arms.

Deedee's eyes went wide. She clung to Hattie's neck, burying her little face. And in a soft, childish, unmistakably clear voice, she said, *"Mama."*

Eight

Luc had known Hattie for a very long time. And he saw the mix of feelings that showed so clearly on her face. Shock. Fierce pride. Joy. Sorrow. Almost too much for one woman to bear, particularly on a day already filled with strong emotion.

He stood and addressed the small group. "Hattie and I are going to slip away for a few moments to spend some time with Deedee before we have to say goodbye. We'll cut the cake when we return. In the meantime, please relax and enjoy the rest of your meal."

He coaxed Hattie out of her seat, witnessing the way she held the baby so tightly to her chest. A crisis was brewing.

In the bedroom where Hattie had changed clothes, his brand-new bride faced him mutinously. "I can't leave her. It's cruel. We'll have to change our plans."

At that moment, Deedee spotted a carry-all stuffed with her favorite toys on the floor in a corner. She wiggled and squirmed and insisted on being put down. Hattie did so with patent reluctance.

Luc tugged Hattie toward the bed and sat her down. "Deedee will be fine. You know it in your heart. Aside from the fact that we need to make our marriage look absolutely real, you need a break, Hattie. Badly. This past year has been one crisis after another. You desperately need to rest and recharge your batteries."

Hattie looked up at him, her lips trembling, her big, brown eyes suspiciously shiny. "She called me *Mama*."

"She certainly did." Luc smoothed her hair where the baby had disheveled it. "And that's what you are."

Hattie bit her lip, not seeming to notice that he was touching her. "I feel guilty," she whispered.

"Why on earth would you say that?"

"I'm happy that Deedee is growing closer to me. I know that's a good thing in the long run. But does that make me disloyal to Angela? How can I be so thrilled that the baby called me *Mama* when she won't even remember Angela, her real mother…"

Luc struggled for wisdom, though he didn't have a good track record when it came to Hattie. "As Deedee grows older you'll show her pictures of your sister.… And later still, you'll explain what happened, when the time is right. Angela will live in your heart, and by your actions, in Deedee's."

"And what about Eddie? What do I tell her about him?"

Luc ground his teeth, unused to feeling helpless in any situation. Did he want to replace Eddie as the baby's father? The temptation was there—he felt it. But he had no desire to be a family man, and Hattie had made it painfully clear that his help was only needed on a temporary basis.

He tried to swallow his frustration. "None of us knows how that situation will work out, but I doubt seriously if Eddie has any interest in being a father. That truth will be hurtful when she's old enough to understand it. But if you've filled her life with love and happiness, Deedee will get through it."

"I hope so," she said softly, her gaze pensive.

He reached out with one hand and touched her bare shoulder, resisting the urge to stroke the satiny skin. "You look beautiful today." The words felt like razor blades in his throat.

Finally, he regained her attention.

A pale pink blush stained her cheeks, and she lowered her head. Her long eyelashes hid her thoughts. "Thank you. I thought this was a better choice than a traditional wedding dress."

Something in her voice made him frown. "Do you regret missing out on a church wedding?"

She shrugged. "I thought I would. It's what many women dream about. But today was…"

"Was what?" he prompted.

She touched his hand briefly, not linking their fingers…more of a butterfly brush. "It was… meaningful."

Her answer disappointed him. He'd hoped for more enthusiasm, more feminine effusiveness. But it hadn't escaped his notice that she'd been careful with the wording of the ceremony. He'd

left that portion of the day in her capable hands.
The printed order of service she'd handed over
on the plane had notably omitted any reference to
"till death do us part" or even the more modern
"as long as we both shall live."

He turned his attention toward the baby, trying
not to notice the way Hattie's rounded breasts
filled the bodice of her gown. She hadn't worn
the pearl necklace today, and the omission hurt
him, though he'd chew glass before he'd admit
it. The only reason he cared was because it was
an outward symbol of the fact that she belonged
to him. She relied on him. She needed him. No
other reason.

He bent and picked up Deedee. "We'd better get
back to our guests. They'll be waiting for cake."

Though the day and the room were plenty
warm, Luc realized that Hattie's fingers were
cold when he put his hand over hers and pressed
down firmly with the knife. Hattie had insisted,
in private, that having a photographer document
their faux wedding was unnecessary. So at the official cake cutting, only Sherman's digital camera
was available to record the moment.

Hattie's smile toward Luc was apologetic as she picked up a small square and pressed it into his mouth. He wasn't sure which he wanted to eat more: the almond-flavored dessert, or her slender, frosting-covered fingertips.

He returned the favor, being careful not to mess up Hattie's makeup or dress. He fed her a tiny piece of cake and then deliberately lifted her hand and licked each of her fingers clean. The guests and servers signaled their approval with a cheer, and Hattie's red-faced embarrassment was worth every penny Luc had spent to make his bride's day special.

Ana stepped forward with a smile. "Shall I help you change clothes, *Mrs. Cavallo?*"

Luc put an arm around Hattie's waist, drawing her closer. He kissed her cheek. "I think we can handle that," he said, his voice low and suggestive.

Once in the bedroom, an irate Hattie rounded on him. "What was that show about? Ana and Sherman know the truth. You embarrassed me."

He shrugged, his hands in his pockets to keep from stripping the deliberately tantalizing dress from her in short order. "The waitstaff and the drivers are outsiders. They may talk, and if they do…I want them to believe that you and I are so much in love we can't keep our hands off each other. Any gossip will help us, not hurt us if they think we're a normal bride and groom."

Hattie stood in the middle of the room, her expression troubled.

He lost his temper. "Oh, for God's sake. I'm not going to jump you when your back is turned. Take off that damned dress and put some clothes on."

She blanched. He felt like a heel. Sexual frustration was riding him hard, and he wondered with bleak mirth what in hell had possessed him to insist on a honeymoon. If his brand-new bride didn't soon admit she wanted him the way he wanted her, he'd be a raving, slobbering lunatic by the time they got back home.

But he couldn't let her think he was affected by the day and the ceremony. The softer, gentler Luc she had known back in college was a phantom. The real Luc was cynical to a fault. What he was feeling was lust, pure and simple. Hattie would be in his bed. Soon. But he wouldn't be weak. Never again. He had his emotions on lockdown.

He turned his back on her and looked out the window blindly, the ocean nothing but a blur. All of his senses were attuned to Hattie's movements. Even when he heard the bathroom door shut, he remained where he was. It was impossible not to imagine her nudity as she stepped out of her bridal attire.

His hands were clammy, and his gut churned.

The bathroom door opened again, and he sighed inwardly. But still he didn't turn around. It was only when Hattie appeared at his elbow that he finally spoke. "Are you ready to go?"

He turned and inhaled sharply. The tiara was gone, her hair was down, but she was still dressed.

She raised a shoulder, her face rueful. "I'm sorry. I can't unzip it. Will you help me?"

God in heaven. She turned her back to him with innocent trust. His hands shook. Inch by inch, as he lowered the zipper, the dress gaped, revealing a sexy piece of fantasy-fueling lingerie. He cleared his throat. "Do you…uh…"

Hattie nodded. "Yeah. The bustier, too."

A million tiny buttons held the confection in place. God knows how long it took him, but he finally succeeded in revealing the pale skin and delicate spine he remembered with such painful clarity. He also remembered running his tongue down that very spine, not stopping until he reached the curve of her ass. And sometimes not even then.

The exercise in torture lasted for what seemed like hours rather than minutes. At last he was finished.

Hattie held the dress to her front with a death grip.

He made himself step back. "All done," he croaked.

She nodded jerkily and scooted toward safety. But just as she reached the bathroom, her toe caught on a scatter rug, she stumbled, and Luc grabbed for her instinctively. His arms went around her from behind and his hands landed in dangerous territory.

Lush, soft breasts. Pert nipples begging to be stroked. He sucked in a breath, sucker punched by the slug of hunger. Hattie froze on the spot like an animal hoping not to be noticed by a hunter.

He nuzzled the nape of her neck. "Your skin is so soft," he muttered. He squeezed gently, cupping the mounds of flesh that he remembered in his dreams.

Her head fell back against his shoulder. "Luc…"

That was all. Just his name. But the single word fraught with what he hoped like hell was longing made him hard as stone and ready for action. He tugged the dress and undergarment from her deathlike grasp and tossed them aside. He couldn't see her face, and he didn't want to.

He continued to play with her breasts slowly. "Tell me you want me, Hattie."

"I want you, Luc…but…"

The last word made him frown. He slid one hand down her belly, between her legs. Hattie gasped audibly.

He bit gently at her earlobe. "But?"

"I don't think we're ready." Her whispered protest barely registered on his consciousness.

He pressed his aching erection against her, her beautiful round butt covered in less than nothing. "Oh, I'm ready, Hattie. Trust me."

The choked laugh she managed made him smile.

At that precise moment, when he felt paradise within his grasp, a loud shout of nearby laughter shattered the moment. They weren't alone. And they had guests waiting.

He cursed in frustration and released her abruptly, wanting to howl at the moon. His timing sucked. "Damn it.… I'm sorry."

Hattie didn't even turn around. He suspected her face was one huge blush. He reached for the discarded clothing and handed it to her. "Go," he said curtly. "We'll deal with this later."

Hattie huddled in the bathroom, her blood running hot and cold in dizzying, equal measure. She had come within inches of shoving her new husband onto the bed and pouncing on him. Feeling his hands on her bare skin had been more arousing than anything she had experienced in the last ten years.

She hadn't been celibate. But still…*holy cow.*

It took her three tries to button her lavender silk blouse. The cream linen trousers she stepped into were part of the outrageously expensive new wardrobe that now filled two large Louis Vuitton suitcases and a garment bag.

She looked in the mirror, wincing at her crazy tousled hair. Nothing to do but to put it up again.

Ana had promised to collect the wedding finery and make sure it got back to the house. So all that was left for Hattie to do was to slip into low-heeled, gold leather sandals and wash her face.

She added fresh lip gloss, took the shine off her nose with a dash of powder, and spritzed her favorite perfume at her throat. What had Luc been thinking as he undressed her? Did he have any feelings left for her at all? Or was it only sex? What if she had turned in his arms and kissed him? Would she have been able to read his face?

He might feel the tug of attraction, but he was no green kid unable to control his body. Hell would probably freeze over before Luc would ever think about having a real relationship with Hattie, whether he saw her naked or not. He liked having her at his mercy. She had invited that with her artless marriage proposal. But Luc was thinking about sex…not a wistful reunion of lovers.

Luc had gained a heck of a lot of sexual experience since they parted. Hattie was old news.

Thinking of the women Luc had probably invited into his bed over the years was a bad thing to do on her wedding day. It only increased her misery. She'd had her chance. And being with

Luc again made her rethink her youthful decision for the umpteenth time. Luc's money gave him power. No doubt about it. But from the perspective of ten years down the road, she admitted ruefully that he wouldn't have used the inequality in their bank accounts to control her, no matter what her mother said.

Her mother's take on life had always been hard-edged. Early disappointments had made her suspicious of people and their motives. Hattie had tried not to follow suit. But perhaps unconsciously that inherent attitude of distrust had been largely to blame for Hattie's breakup with Luc.

When she could procrastinate no longer, she slowly opened the bathroom door. Luc looked up and stared. Something arced across the room between them.

He cleared his throat. "I'll go change now. Why don't you play with the baby? I won't be long."

Before she could respond, he was gone.

Twenty minutes later, amidst the chaos of getting everything and everyone packed up for the return trip, she finally saw her husband again. He was wearing dark slacks and a pale blue dress shirt with the sleeves rolled up. His casual, masculine elegance took her breath away.

It shocked her to realize that she and Luc were not returning on the plane with the rest of the group. And Luc didn't take the time to explain, leaving Hattie to build scenarios in her head, each more unlikely than the next.

Ana stood by as Hattie said one last goodbye to the baby who had become so dear. When Angela was still alive, Hattie had been extremely fond of her tiny niece…as any doting aunt would. But now…now that Hattie played the role of mother, the bond was fierce and unbreakable. She couldn't pinpoint a single instant when it had happened. But the connection was substantial. As much as she was looking forward to spending time with Luc, it pained her to say goodbye to Deedee.

So much was still uncertain. And the baby was so helpless.

Ana patted Hattie's shoulder. "Don't worry… please. We'll watch over her as if she were our own."

Hattie handed over the sleepy child and forced a smile. "I know you will. She adores you and Sherman already. I wouldn't trust her with anyone else." The captain signaled Luc, and Luc began ushering everyone toward the boat.

Leo lingered to speak to Hattie. "I hope you know what you're doing."

She smiled wryly. "Do any of us ever really know what we're doing? I'm trying my best, Leo. It's all I can do."

He hesitated. "Call me if you need anything," he said gruffly. "And be good to my brother."

Before she could respond, he loped toward the end of the dock and boarded the cabin cruiser.

A mournful toot of the horn heralded departure. Luc rejoined Hattie, and they both watched and waved as the vessel moved away from the pilings, picked up speed and slowly skimmed out of sight.

Hattie shifted her feet restlessly. The sun was lower in the sky now, and a breeze had picked up, alleviating some of the heat. "Why didn't we go with them?"

Luc took her arm, leading her back toward the house. "It's been a long, stressful day. I thought it might be nice to relax here for the night. I've ordered a helicopter to pick us up at ten in the morning. He'll take us to the Atlanta airport, and we'll catch our flight to Key West from there."

"Oh."

He must have misread her quiet syllable as lack of enthusiasm, because he frowned. "I'm sorry I'm not taking you somewhere more exotic…like Paris, or St. Moritz. But with Eddie still a loose cannon, I thought it would be wiser to stay where we could get home quickly if need be."

"I think you're right."

Conversation evaporated as they neared the house. Hattie's heart was pounding in her breast. Two people alone on the proverbial deserted island. What happened next?

The truth was anticlimactic. Luc paused on the porch, running a hand through his hair, and for the first time that day, looking uncertain. "Are you hungry at all? We have leftovers."

Hattie had been too nervous earlier to eat much at their wedding meal. "Well, I…"

"It might be nice to sit out on the beach and watch the water while we eat."

Was that a note of coaxing in his voice? She indicated her clothes. "I dressed to travel. Do you mind if I change?"

"Roll up your pants legs. We'll go barefoot and pretend we're teenagers again."

This time there was definitely self-mockery in his words, but she was easily persuaded. They raided the kitchen, and in short order cobbled together a light meal. Luc found a large-handled tote, and they loaded it. Leaving Hattie to carry nothing but two bottles of water, Luc scooped up an old, faded tarp and swung the bag over his shoulder.

She laughed when he kicked off his shoes and rolled his trousers to his knees before they left the house. Following suit, she joined him outside, smiling when she felt the still warm boards beneath her feet.

It was her wedding day. Perhaps an unorthodox one at best, but still deserving of at least a jot of ceremony.

What had happened earlier lingered between them…unspoken, unacknowledged. But it was there, filling her veins with heady anticipation.

Luc managed to spread the ground cloth with her help, though the stiff wind made it necessary to quickly secure the corners with food containers. They sat down side by side. With no baby to act as a shield between them, either literally or figuratively, the mood was much different than it had been during the evening at the park.

Here, on an island far from land, removed from any other humans, it was more difficult to ignore the past.

Luc leaned back on his elbows, his expression pensive. "I wondered about you over the years… what you were doing…if you were happy." He turned his head suddenly and looked straight at her. "Were you?"

"Happy, you mean?"

He nodded.

"It's hard to pin down happiness, isn't it? I had a job that I liked. Friends. Family. So yes, I guess I was happy."

He frowned slightly. "I was an idiot back then. When we were in college. Confusing lust with love. I'm not sure love exists."

Her chest hurt. "How can you not believe in love?"

His gaze returned to the sea. "I understand loving a child, a parent. Those emotions are real. But between men and women?" His lips twisted.

"Mostly hormones, I think. Makes the world go round."

The deliberate cynicism scraped at her guilt. Was that his intention? She curled her legs beneath her, poking at a small crab scurrying in the nearby sand. "You've never come close to marrying before now?"

He smiled faintly. "You mean after the debacle with you? No. Once was enough."

"I'm sorry."

"Don't be. It was a lesson well learned."

She hated his current mood. He was spoiling whatever pleasure she had managed to squeeze from today's events.

Her temper sizzled. Abruptly, she stood up. "I can only apologize so many times. You hate me. I get it. But I can't change the past."

Nine

Luc cursed beneath his breath as Hattie ran from him. Had that been his subconscious intent? To make her angry? So there would be no question of appeasing the ache in his groin?

To say he was conflicted was an understatement. He wanted Hattie with a raw intensity that only increased day by day. But he wasn't willing to give up his position of power. He wouldn't let her see him as a supplicant. It was up to her to come to him. God help him.

He reached into the food bag and found a block of aged cheddar. Not bothering with a knife, he ripped off a hunk and bit into it. The cheese tasted bitter in his mouth. And since he knew all the food at the wedding was top-notch, the problem must be him.

He tossed the uneaten portion back in the bag and went to stand at the water's edge.

Until now, he hadn't allowed himself to think about the men who had shared her life in the intervening years. His fists curled, and he wished violently that he was at the gym so he could beat the crap out of a punching bag.

A swim in the rough surf might appease the beast inside him, but he couldn't take the chance. He wasn't worried about his own safety, but leaving Hattie alone if something happened to him would be the ultimate mark of irresponsibility.

And he was nothing if not responsible.

Damn it. He took off in his bare feet, running full-out, dragging air into his lungs, ignoring the shell fragments that pierced his skin. He kept up the brutal pace, rounding the point and covering mile after mile until he came full circle to where the uneaten picnic lay.

With his chest burning, his feet aching and his skin wind-burned, he stopped suddenly, bent at the waist and rested his hands on his knees. He was used up, worn-out, ready to stop.

But still he wanted Hattie.

Inquisitive gulls had found the bag of food. Much of it would have to be tossed. He waved them away and packed up what he and Hattie had brought to the beach.

The house was quiet and dark when he slipped through the door. He dumped everything in the kitchen and went to his own bedroom, acutely aware that Hattie's was only a few yards away. It was only nine o'clock, but he couldn't see any light from beneath her door.

He stripped off his clothes and took a blisteringly hot shower. The water felt good on his tight, salty skin, but if he had been hoping for a soothing experience, he was out of luck.

His recalcitrant imagination brought Hattie into the glass stall with him. Her generous breasts glistened with soapy water as he washed her from head to toe. His erection was painful. As he stroked himself, he imagined lifting her and filling her, wrapping her long legs around his hips.

Ah.... He came with a muffled groan, slumping at last to sit on the narrow seat and catch his breath. He ran his hands through his wet hair, massaging the pain in his temples.

He was ninety-nine percent sure that Hattie was still sexually attracted to him. And he wanted her in his bed again. But on his terms. She had nearly destroyed him once upon a time. He'd be a fool to let it happen twice. So he'd be on his guard.

Sleep was elusive. Though he'd been up before dawn, he tossed and turned until he finally gave up the pretense of reading and turned out the light. He left the window open, relishing the humid night air. It suited his mood.

The nocturnal sounds were vastly different from back home. Birds and other wildlife filled the night with muted chirps and rustles and clicks. The sea created a hushed backdrop.

At 2:00 a.m. he tossed the tangled covers aside and padded to the kitchen in his boxers to get a drink. The house was dark and silent. He might as well have been the only person on the planet.

He drained the tumbler of water and stepped outside, tempted to run on the beach again. As he moved forward on the boardwalk, his heart stopped. A slender figure in white stood silhouetted against the dark horizon. Hattie. As he closed the distance between them, unconsciously treading as silently as possible, he saw that her back was to him. Her head was lifted to the stars. Her hair danced in the breeze. That same wind plastered her satin nightgown to her shapely body, leaving little to the imagination.

He should have turned back. It was the wise choice. But retreat had never been an option for him. Jump in the deep end, full steam ahead, onward and upward. Pick your cliché—that was how he lived his life. Perhaps if he had handled things differently a decade ago, he might never have lost her.

Something in her posture screamed sadness. And loneliness. An artist would have painted her and titled the canvas *Melancholy*. Seeing Hattie like this cracked something inside him. It hurt.

She didn't flinch when he joined her. Was she as attuned to him as he was to her?

He stood beside her, their shoulders almost touching. Her freshly washed hair was a tangle of damp waves, the light scent of shampoo mingling with the faint fragrance of her perfume.

"Are you okay, Hattie?"

Her chin lowered a bit, her gaze now on the water. She shrugged, not answering in words.

"I was being an ass earlier. I'm sorry."

Her lips twisted. "I should be the one apologizing. I was painfully young and immature back then. I know I hurt you, and I regret it more than you realize. I should have done things differently."

He winced inwardly. She wasn't apologizing for the breakup…only for the way she did it. The distinction was telling.

"I think we're going to have to agree to leave the past where it belongs. We're different people now."

"Leo remembers."

"Leo?"

"He threatened to tear me limb from limb if I hurt his baby brother again. He's very loyal."

Luc snorted. "Leo's a pain in the butt when he wants to be. Forget anything he said to you. I don't need his protection. And he's hardly in a position to be giving relationship advice."

"Maybe not, but he loves you very much."

They fell silent. Luc tried to steady his breathing, but the longer he stood beside her, so close that her warmth radiated to him, the more he became aroused.

"You're sad," he accused softly. "Tell me why."

She shifted restlessly from one foot to the other. "It's not exactly the wedding night I dreamed of."

Dangerous territory. "I'm sorry, Hattie. But, hey." He forced a dry chuckle from his throat. "At least there's moonlight, a romantic beach, a million stars. Could be worse."

"Could be raining." She shot back with the famous line from *Young Frankenstein,* and they both burst into laughter.

He couldn't help himself. He touched her. It was a matter of utmost urgency to find out which was softer—the satin, or her skin. At first, all he did was take her chin in his hand. He turned her so that they were face-to-face, their pose and position mimicking that of the wedding ceremony.

Hattie moved restlessly and he dropped his hand. He sighed. "I take it you couldn't sleep?"

"No."

"Me, either. I've never had a wedding night before. Turns out this stuff is pretty stressful."

That coaxed a small smile from her. "At least

you didn't have to contend with a receiving line and five hundred guests."

"Why do people do that? Sounds exhausting."

"I imagine they want to share their happiness with as many people as possible, and they want to express their appreciation to those who made the effort to show up."

"You apparently have given this some thought."

"It's a typical teenage girl fantasy."

"I wish you could have had your dream wedding."

"Can we talk about something else?" The hint of fatigued petulance made him smile. It was so unlike her.

"I could tell you that when I first looked out here, I thought I was seeing a ghost."

She touched his cheek, making him tremble. "I suppose this must seem like a bad dream to you, your whole world turned upside down. And no end in sight. I owe you, Luc."

He put his hand on hers, keeping the connection. "Perhaps I could collect an installment right now." He'd be kidding himself if he didn't admit that this had been his intent all along. Otherwise, he'd have stayed in the house. But he wouldn't force her. "I'm not the groom you would have chosen, and this sure as hell isn't what you expected from a wedding day. But at least we deserve a kiss...don't we?"

His free hand settled at her waist, caressing the satin-covered curve that led to her hip. As far as he could tell, she was bare beneath the seductive piece of lingerie.

Her eyes searched his, and she moved her hand away. Now both of his palms cupped her hips, inexorably pulling her closer. Her breasts brushed his bare chest. Someone moaned.Was it him?

He leaned his forehead on hers. "Do you want me to stop?"

Small white teeth mutilated her bottom lip. "What I want and what is wise are two different things."

He pushed his hips against hers, letting her feel the evidence of his arousal. He was going to pay like hell for this, but he couldn't stop. "I don't really give a damn about what's wise right at this moment."

They were pressed together now, and they might as well have been naked for all the modesty their thin garments afforded. Every hill and plane of her body fit with his like the most exquisite puzzle. Yin to yang. Positive to negative. Male to female.

She slid her arms around his neck.

He shuddered, struggling to keep a rein on his passion. Sexual attraction. That's all it was. Natural male urgency after a stretch of celibacy.

At first, their lips barely met, hardly touched. Some innate caution they both recognized pretended to slow the dance. But the cataclysm was building and nothing could hold it back.

When her small tongue hesitantly traced his bottom lip, he growled and lifted her off her feet. Their mouths dueled, fumbled, smashed together again in reckless, breathless pleasure.

He had never forgotten her taste…sweet, but with a tart bite like an October apple. The month they first met. The time he'd fallen hard.

And speaking of hard. He rubbed his shaft against her soft belly, making her whimper. That sound of feminine longing went straight to his gut, destroying all semblance of sanity.

Again and again he kissed her…throat, cheeks, eyelids, and back to her soft, puffy-lipped mouth. He dropped to his knees and tongued her navel, wetting the fabric and gripping her hips so tightly he feared bruising her.

Her hands fisted in his hair. But she was holding him close, not pushing him away.

The tsunami crashed over him, an unimagined, unexpected wave of yearning so endless, his eyes stung.

But the aftermath was devastation.

He stumbled to his feet when Hattie tore herself from his embrace, her hair wild, her eyes dark and wide.

She held out a hand when he would have taken her in his arms again. "You've got to give me time," she whispered, her voice hoarse. "It's not just me anymore. I have the baby to think about. I can't afford to make another mistake."

"A mistake." He repeated it dumbly, his control in shreds. His soul froze with a whoosh of unbearable coldness. He shrugged, the studied nonchalance taking every ounce of acting skill he possessed. "You'll have to forgive me. I got carried away by the ambience. But you're right. We're both adults. We should be using our heads, not succumbing to moonlight madness. Let's chalk this up to a long day and leave it at that."

Her arms wrapped around her waist. For a moment he could swear she was going to say something of import.

But she didn't. And for the second time that day, she left him.

If Hattie slept at all, it was only in bits and snatches. Her eyes were gritty when the alarm went off at eight-thirty. And the fact that she had set an alarm for the first morning of her honeymoon made her want to laugh hysterically. She bit down on the macabre humor, afraid that if she let loose of the tight hold she had on her emotions that she would dissolve into a total mess.

She was dressed, packed and sitting on the bed by nine-fifteen. There was plenty of food in the kitchen, but the prospect of eating made her nauseous. Her stomach was tightly knotted, her mouth dry with despair.

When Luc knocked on her door just before ten, she opened it with pseudo calm. "Good morning."

He didn't return her greeting, but merely held out a cup of coffee. It was black and lightly sweet, just the way she liked it. Luc's expression was shuttered, dark smudges beneath his eyes emphasizing his lack of sleep.

As he picked up two of her bags, he spoke quietly. "I can hear the chopper. The pilot and I will load the luggage. Why don't you wait on the porch until we're ready?"

It was all accomplished in minutes. The man flying the helicopter was polite and deferential as he handed Hattie up into the large doorway. Luc followed. They buckled in, the rotors roared to life and moments later they were airborne.

Hattie gazed down at the island and had to blink back tears. It had been a fairy-tale wedding. Too bad she knew that fairy tales were nothing more than pleasant fiction.

The noise in the chopper made conversation impossible. Which was fine by Hattie. She kept her nose glued to the glass and watched the shoreline recede as they cruised across central Georgia. Ignoring Luc at the moment equaled self-preservation.

Landing at Atlanta's enormous airport was frantic. Chaos reigned in controlled waves. Luc gave her a sardonic look as they made their way into the terminal followed by their luggage.

"We're flying commercial today," he said, scanning the departure board for their gate. "I know your Puritan soul would have balked if I had chartered a jet for just the two of us."

The security lines were long and slow. But finally, they were able to board. Hattie had never flown first-class. The width of the seat was generous, but still dangerously close to Luc's. She closed her eyes and pretended to sleep as the jet gathered speed and took off.

Pretense became reality. She woke up only when they touched down in Miami. Luc must have slept, as well, because his usual sartorial perfection was definitely rumpled.

Their connecting flight to Key West was a small plane with only two seats on either side of a narrow aisle. Now she and Luc were wedged hip to hip. After her long nap, it was hard to fake sleep again. So she pretended an intense interest in watching the commotion outside her window.

When they were airborne for the short flight, Luc pulled out a business magazine and buried his head in it.

Hattie and her new groom had barely spoken the entire day.

She was travel-weary, depressed and missing Deedee.

The Key West airport was as tiny as Atlanta's was huge. Nothing more than a handful of plastic chairs and a few car rental counters. Luc had taken care of every detail. Their leased vehicle, a bright, cherry-red convertible, was waiting for them.

The first humorous moment of the day arrived when they struggled to fit their luggage into the car's small trunk. A disgruntled Luc finally conceded defeat and went inside to swap the car for a roomier sedan.

While he was gone, Hattie made a decision. They couldn't ignore each other forever. Last night was a bad mistake. He knew it, and she knew it. So it was best to start over and go from here.

She managed a smile when he returned with the new set of keys. "Sorry that didn't work out. I liked the convertible."

He thrust the last bag into the backseat and motioned for her to get in. "I'd buy you one, but it's not a great car for a mom."

His casual generosity was one thing, but hearing herself called a "mom" shocked her. It was true. She was a mother. The knowledge still had a hard time sinking into her befuddled brain.

Luc had apparently been here before or had at least memorized the route, because he drove with confidence, not bothering to consult the navigation system. When they pulled up in front of a charming two-story structure that looked like a sea captain's home from the nineteenth century, Hattie was surprised and delighted. This was so much better than an impersonal hotel.

The wooden building was painted mint-green with white trim. Neatly trimmed bougainvillea, and other flowers Hattie couldn't name, bloomed in profusion, emphasizing the tropical ambience.

Luc and Hattie had barely stepped from the car when a distinguished gentleman, perhaps in his early sixties, came out to meet them. He extended a hand to each of them. "Welcome to Flamingo's Rest. I'm the innkeeper, Marcel. We have the honeymoon suite all ready for you."

Marcel opened the weathered oak door and ushered them inside.

He grinned at Hattie, clearly happy to be welcoming guests. "You've come at a beautiful time of year."

Marcel led them up carpeted stairs and flung open the door to an apartment that took up half of the second floor. Before Hattie could do more than glance inside, their host smiled broadly. "Key West is the perfect spot for a romantic getaway. Let me know if you need anything at all."

Ten

In the wake of the innkeeper's departure, Hattie watched as Luc prowled the elegant quarters. The bedroom boasted an enormous four-poster king-size bed. Just looking at it through the doorway made Hattie tremble.

At the moment, she was ensconced in less volatile territory. The living area was furnished luxuriously, including a sofa and several chairs, a flat-screen TV, a wet bar and plush carpet underfoot.

Hattie curled up in one of the leather chairs. "This is very nice," she said, her words carefully neutral.

A brief knock at the door heralded the arrival

of their luggage. Marcel and a younger employee stowed everything in the generous closets, accepted Luc's tip with pleased smiles and exited quietly.

In the subsequent silence, awkwardness grew.

Hattie waved a hand, doing her best to seem unconcerned. "I'll sleep out here. The couch is big and comfortable. I'll be fine." She tried changing the subject. "I'm going to call Ana now and see if I can talk to Deedee." She stopped and grinned wryly. "Well, you know what I mean. Do you want to say anything?"

Luc grabbed a beer from the fridge, his movements jerky. "Not right now. I have some business calls I need to make. I'll be in the bedroom if you need me."

Hattie choked on a sound that wasn't quite a giggle. She couldn't help it. After last night, his careless comment struck her as darkly funny.

Luc grimaced, his gaze flinty. "Give Ana and Sherman my regards."

Hattie sighed as he disappeared. Luc was definitely disgruntled. She didn't really blame him. Men didn't do well with sexual frustration, and Hattie herself was feeling out of sorts. What would it take to coax him back into a less confrontational mood?

Deedee chortled and babbled when Ana held the phone to the baby's ear. But Hattie couldn't really tell if Deedee recognized her voice. When the call ended, she had to wipe her eyes, but she knew that this separation wouldn't harm her niece. It was Hattie who was having a hard time.

The sitting room actually had its own bathroom, so Hattie decided to freshen up. Fortunately, she had kept her personal bag with her, so she didn't have to invade the bedroom. Knowing how airlines could lose luggage, she'd packed a pair of khaki walking shorts and a teal blouse in her carry-on. She changed out of her dress into the more casual clothes, breathing a sigh of relief.

Being Luc Cavallo's wife was going to take some adjustment. Hattie was accustomed to traveling in jeans and sneakers, not haute couture.

Her shoes were in one of the big suitcases, so she padded barefoot to the window and looked out into the courtyard. Two small pools, one behind the other, glowed like jewels in the late afternoon sun. It struck her as she glanced at her watch that she had been married an entire day already.

It was a full hour before Luc reappeared. He, too, had changed, but only into a fresh dress shirt. He had his briefcase in hand and a jacket slung over his shoulder.

Hattie's eyes widened. "What's going on?"

"I have to leave." He didn't quite manage to meet her gaze as he fiddled with his watch strap. "There's a crisis in the Miami office, and I'm the closest man on the ground. Our VP there is supposed to be signing a hot new Latin designer, and apparently things aren't going well."

"You're going to Miami?" She was stunned.

He shrugged into his jacket. "I'll talk to Marcel on the way out. Everyone understands business emergencies. He'll look out for you while I'm gone. Shouldn't be more than twenty-four hours at the most, not enough time for anyone to question our marriage. You'll enjoy the shopping here. And order dinner in if you don't feel like getting out tonight."

"You're leaving me on our honeymoon?" The reality was sinking in. She couldn't decide if she was more angry or hurt.

Luc strode to the door, opened it and looked back, his eyes empty of any emotion. "My life didn't suddenly stop when you came back, Hattie. I've done everything you asked. Deedee is safe. We both know this marriage is temporary. You'll have to make some allowances. I sure the hell am."

She curled up on the massive bed and cried for an hour. Insulting, that's what it was. So what if this wasn't a real marriage? Didn't she deserve at least a *pretend* honeymoon?

And did Luc care so little for her feelings that he could simply desert her after last night?

Her eyes were red and puffy, but she was calm when her cell phone rang at nine o'clock. She didn't recognize the number, though she knew it was an Atlanta area code.

Leo's deep voice echoed on the other end. "I need to talk to my brother. He's not answering his damn phone."

Hattie tucked a strand of hair behind her ear and scooted up on the down pillows. "He's not here, Leo."

"What do you mean he's not there?"

"He left. He's gone. Kaput. Some commotion in the Miami office about a new designer and an important contract."

"What the hell?"

Hattie winced. "I don't know what to say, Leo. He's not here."

Muffled profanity on the other end of the line was followed by Leo's long, audible sigh. "I'm sorry, Hattie. I should have gone to Miami. But I've been tied up with another deal."

"It's not your fault. I'm pretty sure this is his way of showing me he's the boss. Or maybe he's dishing out a bit of payback. He still harbors a lot of anger toward me. And I can't really blame him."

"I'm sure the Miami crisis is real."

"It probably is," she said, her voice dull. "But how many brides do you know who would put up with this? Me? I don't have a choice. He holds all the cards. Good night, Leo."

Luc stood on his balcony, staring out at the ocean and cursing his own stubbornness. He'd handled the business crisis in record time and had been ready to speed back to his lovely wife.

But at the last moment he decided to stay gone overnight. It was important that Hattie understand he wouldn't be swayed by his lust.

They were going to have sex…and soon. But he wasn't a slave to his libido. And he wasn't going to fall at her knees and beg.

The irony didn't escape him. He'd been on his knees on his wedding night. But Hattie's indecision had saved him from making a fool of himself. He was back in the driver's seat.

He wondered what Hattie was doing right now. Was she at a restaurant, where available men were hitting on her? He slammed his fist on the railing and welcomed the pain. Maybe it would clear his head.

In business, he knew that the key to success was always, always keeping the upper hand. Last night had been a bad mistake. He'd allowed Hattie to see how much he still wanted her. And that knowledge was power.

She was supposed to beg *him* for sex, not the other way around. He wasn't in love with her. This gnawing ache in his gut was simple male lust. His last relationship had ended several months ago, and since then work had been all-consuming.

When Hattie showed up on his doorstep, it made sense that he would respond to her strongly, given their past and his recent stretch of celibacy. And it made sense for them to enjoy each other physically as long as they were legally man and wife. But when Deedee's situation was secure, Luc would make it clear that it was time for the two females to go.

Hattie fell into an exhausted slumber somewhere around two in the morning. So she was peeved when Marcel knocked at her suite before nine. But when she opened the door, the man standing there was not Marcel. It was Leo Cavallo. Her brand-new brother-in-law.

She ran a hand through her hair, ruefully aware that she looked a mess. "What are you doing here?"

He seemed unusually somber. "May I come in?"

Her knees went weak. "Oh, God. Is it Luc?" She grabbed his shirt. "Tell me. Is he okay?"

Little yellow dots danced in front of her eyes and the world went black.

When she came to, she was lying flat on her back on the sofa with Leo hovering nearby. He patted her hand. "I'm sorry I scared you. Luc is fine." His gaze was accusatory. "You still love him."

She sat up carefully. "Of course I don't."

"Are you pregnant? Is that why you fainted?"

"Leo. For God's sake. I didn't eat dinner and I haven't had breakfast. I got woozy. End of story."

She stood up carefully and went to the minibar for a Coke. She needed caffeine badly, and she wasn't prepared to wait for coffee to brew. "You still haven't told me why you're here." She shot him a bewildered look.

He shrugged, dwarfing the armchair in which he sat. "When you told me Luc had gone to Miami, it got me to thinking. At the wedding, only a blind man could have missed the fact that Luc still has strong feelings for you...and vice versa. I wasn't the only one who noticed."

"Your imagination is impressive."

"Deny it if you want. But regardless, it's a

crappy thing to do to you…abandoning you on your honeymoon."

"And you've come to tell him that?"

"No. I'm here to get him to sign some papers. They're important, but I wouldn't have bothered him on his honeymoon except for the fact that he apparently doesn't see anything wrong with mixing business with pleasure." He held up his hands. "I'll hang out with you until he gets back."

She shook her head, smiling. "I thought I was the villainess of the piece."

"I've been known to be wrong on occasion." He shrugged, his boyish grin equally as appealing as her husband's. But Leo's smile didn't stir her heartbeat in the least.

"That's sweet of you, but not necessary. I can entertain myself."

"Quit arguing. Go put your swimsuit on. I'll do a quick change myself and get Marcel to roust us up some brunch."

Leo was as good as his word. When Hattie made her way down to the pool in silver slides and an emerald-green maillot, her brother-in-law was already stretched out on a chaise lounge, apparently content to while away a few hours.

As she sat down beside him, she heard a quiet snore. He must have taken the red-eye. Poor guy. She'd let him sleep.

When the sun warmed her through and through, she slipped into the pool with a sigh of pleasure. Being rich definitely had its advantages. She did some laps and then floated lazily, feeling the hot rays beating down on her.

It was nice of Leo to keep her company, but Hattie wanted her husband…stripped down to nothing but his swim trunks so she could ogle his body to her heart's content.

If Marcel thought it odd that a new bride was frolicking poolside with a man who wasn't her husband, he made no sign. He was polite and unobtrusive when he brought out a tray laden with everything from scrambled eggs and bacon to fresh mangoes and homemade croissants filled with dark chocolate.

Leo roused in time to devour his share of the repast. "I was hungry," he said sheepishly as he snitched a lone strawberry.

Hattie lay back, her cup and saucer balanced on her tummy. "This coffee is to die for. I'll have to find out what brand it is." She finished her drink and turned on her stomach…drifting, half-awake, listening to birdsong and the gentle sough of the wind in the palm fronds.

Leo poked her knee. "You're turning pink, princess. Better put some sunscreen on."

Without opening her eyes, she reached for the bottle of lotion under her chair. "Will you do my back, please? I'll throw a towel over my legs, so don't bother with that."

Luc parked the car in front of the B and B and sat for ten seconds, giving himself a lecture. He was calm. He was in control. Hattie would dance to his tune.

He had a plan. One that would satisfy the hunger riding him and at the same time make it clear to his new wife that nothing had changed. Their marriage was still temporary.

It was an unpleasant shock to find their suite empty. But then he took a deep breath. Hattie was shopping, that was all. Women loved to shop. The tourist district of Key West wasn't all that big. Maybe he would take the car and drive around for a bit, see if he spotted her.

As he hurried back down the stairs, keys in

hand, Marcel intercepted him. "Welcome back, Mr. Cavallo. I hope your business was transacted successfully."

"Yeah," Luc muttered, unaccountably embarrassed. "Do you happen to know if Hattie has gone to town?"

Marcel shook his head. "Your wife is out by the pool with her friend. I served them a meal not long ago. Shall I bring more food?"

"No thanks. Not hungry."

Luc's hackles rose. *Her friend?* No doubt, some handsome surfer type had taken advantage of Luc's short absence to make a move.

Well, not for long, buddy.

Luc walked outside, keeping behind the bushes until he got a clear shot of the pool. Hattie was stretched out, facedown, in a suit that made his mouth water. But the sight that took his breath away was the large man rubbing lotion into Hattie's shoulders.

Damn and double damn. The guy had his back to Luc, and at this distance, Luc couldn't really tell much about him…except that he was getting way too chummy with Luc's wife.

The man murmured something to Hattie that

made her laugh. Luc's vision blurred with rage and indignation.

He burst through the shrubbery and advanced on the couple by the pool. "What in the hell is going on?"

The man turned his head and smiled...a wicked, *look what I'm up to* smile. Leo stood up. "Well, hello, Luc. It's about damn time you got here."

Though he was stunned, Luc didn't let on. "Why are you here, Leo? If you're dying for a honeymoon, find your own damn wife."

Leo mocked him deliberately. "When I heard that you were willing to transact business this week, I brought some contracts that need your John Hancock ASAP."

By this time, Hattie had scrambled to her feet. Her sweat-sheened breasts revealed by the relatively modest décolletage of her suit gave Luc pause for a second or two, but he dragged his eyes away from his wife's erotic body and faced off with his sibling.

Luc looked pointedly at Leo's casual attire. "But nothing so urgent that you couldn't chill out by the pool," he said, irritated beyond belief.

It had been years since he and Leo had tangled in a fistfight, but Luc was spoiling for a rematch.

Hattie grabbed his arm. "Sit down, Luc. You're being rude."

Leo egged him on. "It's your fault, little bro. I wouldn't be here if you hadn't been such a Type A jerk."

That was it. Luc lunged at Leo, determined to pummel him into the ground. Their bodies collided and the fight was on.

But Luc hadn't counted on Hattie.

She grabbed his shirt and clung to him. "Stop this. Right now. You're both insane."

He shrugged her off. "Get out of the way." He rammed his shoulder into Leo's chest. Leo fired back with a punch to Luc's solar plexus.

Hattie jumped on Luc's back this time, her arms around his neck in a stranglehold. "I mean it," she pleaded, her voice shaking. "He's your brother."

A second time Luc shook her off. "He's a pain in the ass."

Leo was momentarily distracted by Hattie's distress. Luc used the brief advantage to land another right to Leo's chin, this time splitting his own knuckles.

Hattie tried a third intervention, grabbing Luc's belt with two hands. But both men were in motion and when she lost her grasp, she slipped on the wet surface of the pool deck and fell sideways, her cheek raking the edge of the glass-topped table as she went down.

Luc and Leo froze. Luc was down on his knees in seconds, scooping her into his arms. "Oh, God, Hattie. Are you okay?"

She struggled to a sitting position and said, "Yes."

But she was lying. Blood oozed down her cheek from a nasty gash.

Leo crouched with them, cursing beneath his breath. "Is it bad?"

"I can't tell," Luc said, his hands shaky. "We need to get her checked out."

Hattie waved a hand. "Hellooo. I'm right here. If you two doofuses would kiss and make up, I'll be fine."

Luc eyes his brother sheepishly. "Sorry, man."

Leo grinned. "I deserved it."

Hattie rolled her eyes. "Morons." Luc heard rueful affection in the two syllables.

He motioned to his brother. "Grab one of those cloth napkins."

Leo complied, wetting the fabric in a water glass.

When Luc pressed gently at the wound, Hattie winced. "That hurts. Let me do it."

He surrendered the makeshift swab reluctantly, watching in dismay as Hattie removed more of the blood. It was an odd cut, and one that stitches wouldn't necessarily help.

The unflappable Marcel appeared, handing over a first aid kit. He glanced quickly at Hattie's cheek. "A butterfly bandage should do the trick, I think."

Luc applied antibiotic ointment and pressed the plaster in place as tenderly as he could. He and Leo helped her to her feet.

Now that the immediate crisis was over, Hattie was clearly flustered. She reached for her sheer cover-up and slid her arms into it. "I'm going upstairs to take a shower," she said, her eyes daring him to protest. "I suggest you two get your act together while I'm gone."

She turned with dignity to Marcel. "Thank you for your help. It's nice to know that someone around here has good sense."

As she flounced her way into the house, Leo shook his head and smiled. "Your wife is one tough cookie."

Luc nodded, sobered by what might have been. "For once, I agree with you completely."

Eleven

When Hattie stepped into the sitting room, she saw Luc ensconced on the sofa, elbows on his knees, waiting for her.

He stood and faced her. "You look nice."

She picked up her purse, fiddling with the contents. "Thanks." She was wearing a gauzy ankle-length dress in shades of taupe and gold. It was sleeveless, and the V neck dipped low front and back. A necklace and bracelet in chunky amber stones complemented the outfit.

The small bandage on her cheekbone made her self-conscious, but that was mostly vanity talking. Her ensemble was dressy but comfortable.

After the last few days, relaxation was high on Hattie's list.

She bit her lip, not wanting to resurrect any bad feelings. "Where's Leo?"

Luc made a face. "Don't worry. I signed the damn papers. He's changing downstairs to give us some privacy. I thought we'd go out for a late lunch somewhere nice, and afterward, he'll head home."

Leaving us all alone on our "it-has-to-get-better-than-this" honeymoon. The thought swept through Hattie's brain like wildfire, singeing neurons and making her legs weak. "Sounds good."

But when they got downstairs, Leo was gone. Marcel handed over a note. Luc read it, his expression blank and then passed it over to Hattie.

Don't want to intrude. Have a good week. See you in Hotlanta.

Hattie tossed the little piece of paper in a nearby trash can, her palms damp. "I guess it's just us."

Luc's gaze was hooded. "Guess so."

He ushered her out to the car, and they drove the short distance to the historic district. After squeezing into a tiny parking space on a street curb, Luc shut off the engine and came around to open Hattie's door. His hand on her elbow did amazing things to her heart rate.

She told herself not to expect too much. Nothing had changed. They weren't a normal couple by any means.

But it was hard to remember such mundane considerations amidst the tropical atmosphere of Key West. Everyone was in a good mood, it seemed. And no wonder. The view from Mallory Square was filled with cerulean seas, colorful watercraft and white, billowing triangles atop sailboats that zigged and zagged across the open waves.

Just offshore lay a palm-fringed island that looked so perfect Hattie wondered if the Chamber of Commerce had painted it against the sky to frame the sunsets.

When she said as much, Luc responded. "One of the large hotel chains owns it. You can rent one-, two- or three-bedroom cottages, and they even have their own man-made beach."

Hattie had already realized that Key West was not a typical "beach" destination. The coastline was rocky or coral-built. The Conch Republic, as it was called, was literally the last stop before Cuba, a mere ninety miles southwest.

At a marina adjacent to one of the fabulous hotels, Luc took Hattie's hand and helped her down into a sleek speedboat. Moments later, they were cutting across the waves, bound for the island.

In minutes, they pulled up to a well-kept dock and stepped out of the boat. A uniformed attendant directed them to the restaurant. It was open air on three sides, with huge rattan ceiling fans rotating overhead as an adjunct to the natural sea breezes. Delicate potted orchids bloomed on each table. China, silver and crystal gleamed.

The food was amazing…fresh shrimp gumbo and homemade corn bread. Hattie chewed automatically.

She was ready for a showdown, but if she initiated what might turn out to be a shouting match, would it be worth it? Hattie's mother had made a life's work out of tiptoeing around Hattie's stepfather. She always acted as if he might desert her at any moment.

The truth was that the guy loved Hattie's mother and would have given her anything. But early lessons are hard to unlearn. Hattie wasn't proficient at confrontation, but then again, she was no pushover. Luc was doing her a favor, yes. But that didn't mean he could dominate her.

She waited until the server put a piece of key lime pie in front of each of them before she fired the first shot. "How was your business trip?"

Luc choked on a bite of dessert. "Fine," he muttered. "This pie is great."

She wouldn't be deterred. If she had been clearer about her feelings a decade ago, she and Luc might possibly have worked things out. Her jaw tightened. "There was no excuse for you to leave on the first day of our honeymoon. Not only was it disrespectful to me, it also endangered our pretense of a happy marriage. I think you were trying to teach me a lesson, but it backfired."

Luc set down his fork and leaned back in his chair, his face sober. He exhaled slowly, his lips twisted. "You're right, of course. And I do apologize."

She cocked her head, studying him, trying to see inside his brain. "I've never said this, but my leaving you wasn't really about money. It was about control."

Luc jerked as if she had slapped him. "I don't understand."

"As a young woman, my mother had an affair with her boss, a wealthy, powerful man. When she told him she was pregnant, he cast her off without a second thought. That shining example of a man was my father. My biological father."

Shock creased his face. "I wasn't your boss, Hattie. What does that have to do with anything? I feel sorry for your mother, but you're certainly not the kind to do something so reckless."

"You're missing the point. My whole childhood revolved around this missing mystery man. This terrible person who didn't want me. And to hear my mother tell it, money was what gave him all the power. Leaving her power*less* and alone. From the time I was old enough to understand, she drilled into me the importance of making my own way in the world and not letting any man control my destiny."

"And you thought I would do something like that to you?" He looked haunted.

"Of course not. But I was so head over heels in love with you, I was afraid I'd lose myself in your life. It's very easy to be taken care of, very addictive. And I wasn't brave enough to stick with you. In hindsight, I believe I was stronger than I realized at the time. But as a kid of twenty, all I could see was that you had the money and power to do anything you wanted. And I felt lost in your shadow."

"Despite the fact that I wanted you so badly I followed you around like a puppy."

"You were a young man at the mercy of his hormones. Sex makes men do crazy things."

They were sitting at adjoining corners of a table for four. Beneath the linen cloth, Luc took her hand and deliberately pushed it against his erection. "I'm not so young now," he growled, releasing her fingers and eating his pie as if nothing had happened.

The imprint of his rigid flesh was burned into Hattie's palm. She took a reckless swallow of wine. "Don't be crass."

He shrugged, his eyes a dangerous flash of obsidian. "What do you want from me, Hattie?"

She hesitated, torn between fascinated curiosity about his response to her and a healthy sense of caution. "Do you really think we can be intimate and then walk away?"

Luc shrugged again. "I can if you can."

Hattie frowned, licking whipped cream from her spoon. His nonchalance could be an act. Her heart beat faster.

She cocked her head and stared at him, trying to read his mind. He was as inscrutable as the great and powerful wizard of Oz. If Hattie could click her heels in ruby slippers, she'd be able to go back to that innocent time in college.

Did she want to? Or did she want to move ahead as an adult woman with adult needs? She'd be taking an enormous risk. What if she fell in love with Luc again? What if she never had really *stopped* loving him? What if they had sex and it was ho-hum?

Not likely.

She scraped one last bite of topping from her plate and ate it absently. Luc's hungry gaze followed every motion she made. Her throat dried. It was now or never.

When the waiter moved to a safe distance, Hattie rested her arms on the table and moved in close to Luc. She put her hand over his. "You said I had to be the one to say yes or no. But you have to know that my answer has nothing to do with protecting a baby…nothing to do with mistakes we made in the past. No feelings of obligation. This is about us…you and me. And I say—"

Luc put his hand over her mouth, his expression violent. "Not another word."

Luc was burning up. The tropical heat and Hattie's proximity made him sweat. Her gaze seemed to dissect him like a bug. To burrow inside his brain and discern his secrets. He lifted an impatient hand for the check, deliberately breaking their physical connection. He was too close to the edge. Hearing Hattie acquiesce to their mutual desire for sexual intimacy could push him over. And it wouldn't be smart to let her realize how desperate he was to have her. Talking about sex in a public venue had not helped in the least when it came to controlling his baser urges.

After he shoved two large bills into the folio, he took Hattie by the wrist, dragging her toward the exit. "We're going back to the house," he said. "I think you have sunstroke."

She laughed softly. They reached the dock, and it was all he could do not to crush her against one of the wooden posts and ravage her mouth with his. He damned the surroundings that forced him to act like a gentleman. He'd never felt less civilized in his life.

Other tourists joined them beneath the awning, and soon the return boat arrived. Hattie's hip and thigh were glued to Luc's in the small, crowded craft. Back on dry land, she followed him meekly to the car. Her honey-blond hair gleamed in the unforgiving sun.

Seeing her pink shoulders made him think of Leo again. Which made him think of doing the lotion thing for Hattie, covering every inch of her creamy skin with fragrant moisture.

He knew what she was going to say, and his body said a resounding *"hell, yeah!"* But in addition to his need to remain in control, it occurred to him that he owed her some romance… to make up for his less than stellar behavior as a new groom. They had eight or nine hours to kill before bedtime. It was far too hot to walk the streets in the midday heat.

Fortunately, their rental was parked beneath a huge shade tree. Luc leaned his elbows on the top of the car and faced Hattie with the vehicle between them. "What would you like to do now?" he asked, wishing he could supply the answer.

She lifted the hair from the back of her neck and sighed. "I love the pool," she said. "Do you mind too much if we go back and swim? We can play tourist tomorrow."

"Whatever you want," he croaked, his mind racing ahead. Swimming as foreplay made as much sense as anything else to his testosterone fuddled brain.

In the bedroom there was an awkward moment when they both reached into suitcases with plans to change clothes. Luc held up his hands, gripping a pair of black swim trunks. "I'll use the other bathroom."

He was ready in four minutes. It took Hattie an extra twenty. But when she reappeared, he wasn't about to complain. Her hair was swept up on top of her head, leaving recalcitrant tendrils to cling to her damp neck. The white terry robe she wore covered her from throat to knee, but it molded to her breasts and hips with just enough cling to encourage his imagination.

He thought he had himself under control. But all bets were off when they reached the pool and

Hattie ditched the cover-up. She wore a different suit this time, and he was damned glad Leo hadn't been around to see this one.

It was a neon-blue bikini. Luc was stunned. She was a sexual goddess, even more lovely than she had been in college. The bikini bottom fastened at the hips with a large gold circlet on either side. The two tiny triangles of fabric that made up the top barely met decency standards.

Luc looked around suspiciously to see if anyone else was enjoying the show, but their privacy was absolute. Nothing but flowers and water and a mermaid just for his entertainment. If there were other guests at the small inn, they were not around at the moment.

Luc made a show of selecting a chaise lounge and flipping out his towel. "I'm going to nap."

Hattie gazed at him over her shoulder, her eyes hidden behind tortoiseshell sunglasses. "Will you do me first?"

His body went rigid in shock until he saw the bottle of sunscreen she held out. "Sure."

When she was situated, he perched on his hip beside her and unscrewed the lid. Immediately, the scent of coconut assailed his nostrils. Hattie pillowed her head on her arms, a small smile tilting her lips.

Luc groaned inwardly. Giving her a taste of romance before the main event might drive him mad.

When his hands touched her back, she flinched. "It's cold."

He ran his fingers across her shoulder blades. "It won't be. Relax."

Too bad he couldn't take his own advice. Every one of his muscles was tight enough to snap. He exhaled slowly and concentrated on Hattie. His fingertips still remembered the hills and valleys of her body. His thumbs pressed on either side of her spine.

Hattie moaned.

Dear Lord.

When he hesitated, she lifted a hand and waved it lazily, her eyes closed. "Don't stop."

He smoothed one final spot of lotion into her skin and capped the bottle. "All done."

Hattie didn't answer. She was so still he suspected she had drifted off. Which irked him, because sleep was the furthest thing from his mind. He stood up and went to the deep end of the pool. After one last glance at Hattie, he dove in and started a series of punishing laps. Harder and faster, pushing his body to exhaustion.

He swam until his legs began to feel like spaghetti. And then he swam some more. When spots of light began to dance behind his eyelids, he dragged himself out of the pool and collapsed onto his lounger facedown. Hattie lay where he had left her, her almost naked body lax and limp, her skin glistening with a dewy sheen of lotion and perspiration.

Luc closed his eyes, his heart pounding in his chest. He had a painful erection. His body was clenched with desire, despite the brutal workout. He was a man, not a eunuch. He might not be in love with Hattie like he'd been as a stupid kid of twenty, but he had normal male needs. If she didn't come to him soon, he'd never be able to keep up the pretense that he was in control of the situation.

It was a shock to feel hands on his back. He'd been so caught up in his own turmoil, he never heard Hattie move. She mimicked his earlier position and was now preparing to rub sunscreen into his burning skin. Thankfully, his Italian heritage made him able to endure the sun without painful consequences, but he knew he needed the protection.

The question was—who or what would protect him from Hattie?

Her hands were small, but strong. Despite the ostensible point of the exercise, this was foreplay. And Luc was strung so tightly, he wasn't sure he could bear it.

Five minutes later, his body aching with the need to roll over and pull Hattie down into his arms, she finished. He felt her touch on his hair, her fingers ruffling the wet strands.

She leaned in closer, her breast brushing his side. "I'm getting in the water. Why don't you join me?"

It was a dare. He recognized it as such and knew that this game of cat and mouse had only one possible conclusion. But it was up to him to write the script and make sure Hattie knew who was in control.

He swung to a sitting position. Now they were so close, he could have leaned forward a scant two inches and kissed her. But he didn't. Not yet.

He smiled grimly, cursing his body's weakness. "After you."

She didn't try to dive in, but instead used the

ladder to lower herself into the pool. The water was only chest high where she stood. He executed a show-off dive from the opposite direction and came up beside her, shoving the hair from his face. Her eyes were wide.

He touched her shoulder. "Want a ride in the deep end?"

Hattie nodded, not speaking.

He took her hand. "Get on my back."

When she complied, her legs wrapping around his waist and her arms encircling his shoulders, he shuddered. "Hang on."

He walked forward, feeling the bottom of the pool fall away beneath his feet. When he could barely touch bottom, he tugged her off his back and around until she faced him. The slightly surprised look in her eyes when she realized she was out of her depth made him smile inwardly.

Her hands clenched his shoulders, her fingernails leaving marks in his skin. Their legs drifted together and apart. He knew she felt the evidence of what she did to him.

Hattie nibbled her bottom lip. "The water feels great."

She was nervous. He liked that. "A lot of things feel great," he said, deliberately taunting her.

"You didn't let me give you my answer earlier," she said, her eyes alight with mischief.

He kissed her softly, a bare brush of mouth to mouth. She tasted like warm summer fruit. "It will keep," he muttered. "No need to rush."

Need swam between them. His. Hers. It might have been a decade, but some pleasures the body never forgets.

Her eyes drifted shut.

"No. Look at me." He cupped one breast.

Hattie's eyelids fluttered open, her gaze unfocused, her cheeks flushed despite the cool water. Her soft cry went straight to his gut.

He kicked his legs rhythmically, keeping them afloat. Now he took the other breast. Two handfuls...warm, seductive, feminine bounty. He massaged gently, moving the barely-there bikini top aside to find naked flesh.

The pleasure flooding him from touching her so intimately blurred his vision. His hands settled at her waist as he took her mouth in a ravaging kiss. They were in danger of losing all rational thought. And he was sinking fast.

As fact matched thought, they slipped beneath the surface of the water. He kissed her again, and this time, he slid his hand into the bottom of her bikini and cupped her, pressing a finger into her tight passage and probing…stroking.

It lasted no more than a few seconds. He dragged them both back up for air. Hattie wrapped her legs around his waist, her ragged breathing matching his. She had a death grip on his shoulders, her breasts mashed to his chest.

She initiated the kiss this time, her small teeth nipping his bottom lip, her tongue sliding between his teeth, dazing him with an ache so intense, his head hurt. Hunger raged like a wild animal, one that hadn't been fed in a decade.

She whimpered when he cupped her bottom, pulling her closer. "Luc…Luc."

Hearing his name on her lips almost unmanned him. "What, Hattie?"

"Please," she groaned. "My answer is yes. Please, please, please make love to me."

Exultation filled his chest. That was what he needed to hear. "Ask me again," he demanded.

Her gaze filled with frustration. "No games. Take me. Now."

Twelve

Hattie stumbled as Luc dragged her toward the house, their few belongings left behind in his haste. His grip on her wrist allowed no protest. But then why would she…protest, that is?

She wanted Luc—the sooner the better.

If she had expected awkwardness in the bedroom, she was wrong. Luc was smooth, determined. He stripped off his trunks, grinning tightly when she looked her fill.

His erection was magnificent. Thick, long and ready for her…only her. His broad chest and strong arms rippled with muscles. He cupped her face in his hands. "Take it off."

His adamant tone brooked no refusal.

She trembled inside and out as she unfastened the knot at the back of her neck and reached behind to undo the clasp. For seconds, the bikini top clung damply to her breasts as she clutched it in sudden, belated hesitation.

The corner of Luc's beautiful mouth quirked in a half smile. "Don't go all shy on me now, Hattie."

She gulped inwardly and let the scraps of fabric fall. Luc inhaled sharply. The look in his eyes made her weak. In college, he had been her first love, her first lover. Now he was a mature man in his sexual prime. She felt the heat of his desire, not as quiet warmth, but as a flashpoint poised to explode.

There was the problem of what to do with her hands. She wanted to cover her breasts instinctively. But she knew Luc would have none of that. So her arms hung at her sides as she shifted from one foot to the other.

He lifted an eyebrow. "You're not finished."

She might have taken umbrage at his arrogant tone had she not been as eager as he was for the next act. Removing her last barrier of modesty proved harder than she expected.

Luc lost patience. He gripped her hips. "Too slow," he growled. He kissed her wildly, his mouth everywhere…her lips, her throat, and finally, her bare breasts. The sensation was an electric shock. Her entire body melted into him, closer and closer still.

His hard shaft bruised her hipbone. The soft, wiry hair on his chest tickled her sensitive skin. Breath by gasping breath they relearned the taste of each other—the touch, the sound, the smell. It was a smorgasbord of sensual delight. A cornucopia of excess.

He tangled his fingers in the rings at her hips and jerked hard, ripping the thin fabric from the metal. The remnants that he tossed aside represented Hattie's last resistance, if indeed she had any.

She was drunk on memories laced with present passion.

A nanosecond later he lifted her. Her legs wrapped around his waist instinctively. The intimate position made her limp with longing. He backed her up to the nearest wall and buried his face in her neck. Tremors shook his large frame. His chest heaved.

Slowly, as if giving her time to protest, he aligned their bodies and entered her with one forceful upward thrust. He was big, but she was ready for him. When he was buried inside her, he went still.

"Hattie?" His voice was hoarse.

"Hmmm?" She bit his earlobe and heard him curse.

"You okay?"

The four-letter word didn't come close to describing what she was. "Don't stop."

"Whatever the lady wants."

The last words were barely audible as he directed all his energy toward driving them both insane. Her bare butt slapped against the door as Luc pounded into her over and over.

A searing heat built inside her, coalesced at the spot where their bodies were joined. Higher. Stronger. The world ceased to exist. Her arms tightened around his neck as she felt the storm begin to break. "Luc…" Stars cartwheeled inside her head and tumbled downward to reignite when Luc's own release sent him rigid and straining against her.

When it was over at last, Luc staggered into

their bedroom, still carrying her, and dropped her onto the mattress. He came down beside her and rested his head on her chest.

Her heart stopped. A perfect cocoon of intimacy enveloped them.

She might have slept for a few minutes—she wasn't sure. Luc was out, his body a heavy weight half on top of her. She wanted so badly to stroke his hair, but she resisted. A black hole of self-destruction yawned at her feet. She was far too close to the edge.

Awkwardly, she slid from beneath him and tip-toed to the bathroom. After quickly freshening up, she put on one of the soft luxurious robes that hung on the back of the door. Belting it tightly, she peeked out into the bedroom.

Luc's speculative gaze met hers. "You won't need the robe."

Five simple words. That's all he needed to make the moisture bloom between her legs. She grasped the door frame to steady herself. "I won't?" All the starch had left her legs. She was melting, body and soul.

He crooked a finger. "Come back to bed."

Removing the robe was even more difficult

than shedding her swimsuit. In the heat of the moment, her inhibitions had gone on vacation. But now they were back.

As she padded into the room, shivering, she noticed for the first time that the AC had been kicked up a notch. Luc held a string of condom packets in his hand. "We skipped a step. I'm sorry, Hattie. That was my fault."

She shrugged with what she hoped was blasé sophistication. "It's the wrong part of the month. I'm not worried."

His grin was tight. "Then let's not waste any more time."

The robe fell at her feet. Luc's amusement faded visibly to be replaced by sheer male determination. When she shivered now, it had nothing to do with the temperature in the room and everything to do with the man stretched out on his back like a sleek, not-quite-satisfied predator.

Nothing this older, more experienced Luc did was predictable. Instead of covering her with his aroused body, he pulled her on top. It was a position she had never really liked, because it made her feel too vulnerable. But when she tried to protest, Luc took care of that by lightly touching the small bud of nerves at her center.

She braced her hands on her thighs and tried not to flinch as he explored her most private recesses. In an embarrassingly short amount of time, she moaned and climaxed, the second event no less powerful than the first.

He held her close and stroked her hair, though she could feel the strength of his unappeased desire. Tears clogged her throat. "Luc, I…" *love you.* No, she didn't. It was just the sex talking. Shades of auld lang syne. An overabundance of postcoital hormones.

He kissed her cheek. "You what?"

"I wonder if we made a mistake." She felt him go still.

"Regrets already?"

Something in his tone made her cringe. She shouldn't have introduced reality into their bed. Not now. But she was compelled to answer. "This makes things complicated. When we go our separate ways."

His hands moved from her hair, her shoulders. He shifted her until they lay side by side. Already she missed his warmth.

His tone was perfectly calm when he answered. "You're making too much of nothing. There's no harm in enjoying each other. Divorces are simple nowadays. We'll deal with any complications when we have to. It's nothing to worry about."

She winced inwardly, her lovely moment shattered by her own bad timing and Luc's carelessly callous comment. No more pretending. This wasn't a honeymoon. This was sex for the sake of scratching an itch. No use dressing it up with romantic frills.

No reason for tears to sting her eyes and a painful lump to clog her throat.

She swallowed, her mouth dry. "I want to take a shower."

Luc pounced verbally. "No, Hattie. I don't think so."

He hardly noticed that she didn't answer. He'd been kicked in the gut and was left reeling. The sweat was barely dry on their bodies and she was already talking about leaving him. Damn it to hell. *He* would be the one to end this relationship…not Hattie.

He was hard as a pike, his erection painfully

stiff. With jerky motions, he ripped open a packet and rolled on a rubber. A split second later he groaned aloud as he penetrated Hattie's tight, wet warmth. She lay passive beneath him, and it pissed him off.

He took her chin in his hand. "Look at me, Mrs. Cavallo." She obeyed. He had to grit his teeth to keep from coming right then. "What we do in the privacy of our bed is our own business. We're good together. Don't fight it. Don't fight me. Let yourself go, Hattie."

Big brown eyes looked up at him with a mixture of emotions he couldn't decipher even if he wasn't being driven by his baser needs. She whispered the single word. "Okay."

It was enough. He felt her hands touch his hips, recognized the moment when she arched her back and matched her rhythm to his. A red haze clouded his vision. His hips pistoned in agonized yearning for release. It was good…so good.

Hattie gave a small shocked cry as he felt her inner muscles squeeze him. Her release triggered his, and he bore down, losing himself in her welcome embrace and finding momentary oblivion.

* * *

Sometime later, sanity returned. He could hear his own jerky breathing in the silence of the room. Hattie was still and quiet again. Had he hurt her? He moved aside with a muttered apology, relieving her of his considerable weight.

Sweet mother of God. He hadn't had sex that good in he didn't know when. *Oh, yes, you do. It was back in college when Hattie was warm and willing and you were both blissfully happy.*

He shook off the memories. No need for those when he had the real thing in his arms. What was she thinking? He was too tired to pry it out of her. He'd barely slept the night before.

His eyes closed involuntarily.

Aeons later it seemed, he felt her try to escape. His fingers closed around her wrist. "Stay."

"I need a shower."

He scrubbed his hands over his face, yawning, his head muzzy. "I'll join you."

The look on her face made him laugh as he got to his feet. "Don't be so modest. It's the green thing to do."

After turning the water to a comfortable temperature, he dragged a clearly reluctant Hattie into the luxurious shower enclosure. His lovely new wife huddled in a tiled corner, her arms wrapped around her waist.

Everything about her screamed innocent seduction…from her long slender legs to her hourglass waist, to her plump, shapely breasts. If he could paint, he'd commit her to canvas exactly like this.

He picked up a bar of soap shaped like a shell. "Turn around."

Hattie was drowning in her own need. In her wildest imagination she had never invented a scenario like this. "Why?" she muttered.

His grin was lethal. "I thought you wanted to get clean."

"You're a dirty old man."

"Not old," he deadpanned.

She gave him her back reluctantly, hyperaware that she was at his sexual mercy. The first touch of the washcloth made her jump. But it was Luc's chuckle that made her blush.

As he washed from her neck down her spine, she braced her hands on the wall and hung her head. Luc had turned the spray so that it cascaded between them. The water was cool on Hattie's hot skin.

Luc moved the rag slowly, more of a massage than a simple exercise in cleanliness. He reached her bottom and squeezed. "Turn around."

She obeyed instinctively, their gazes colliding amidst the steamy air. "I can do the rest," she said.

He shook his head. "Why bother? I'm off to a hell of a good start." He took her hands and tucked them behind her butt. "Don't move."

The hot water was enervating, draining Hattie of any will to challenge Luc's control. This time he made no pretense of using the washcloth. He took the bar of soap and ran it in circles around her breasts. Then he pressed gently over her nipples, decorating them with tiny bubbles.

When he was satisfied, he paused to kiss her… slow and deep. With one hand, he manacled her wrists behind her back with a firm grip. Now their bodies were touching chest to chest. She felt his erection throbbing between them.

He nuzzled her nose with his and ground his hips into hers. "More work to do," he muttered.

His hand holding the soap found its way south

to the middle of her thighs. Her legs parted instinctively to give him access.

When the soap glided over a certain sensitive spot, Hattie cried out and struggled. But Luc kept his tight hold on her wrists as he moved the soap between her legs.

Hattie rested her forehead on his chest, panting. "Enough," she whispered. "I'm clean." She was close to the edge, but she didn't want to make the journey alone. She wanted Luc inside her, filling her, making her his.

Without warning, he dropped the soap and released her wrists. The shower boasted a roomy stone seat. Luc reached for the condom he'd tucked on a ledge, sheathed himself, and then pulled Hattie down to sit astride his lap.

Their bodies were slick and wet, and the moment when they joined was seamless...easy. Hattie threw back her head, the water still streaming over them. Her eyes were closed, intensifying the sensation of having Luc inside her.

He was strong. He lifted her up and down in a gentle rhythm, teasing them both.

Longing crescendoed, hunger peaked. Luc's hands bruised her bare butt as he gave a muffled shout and found his release. Hattie still lingered on the knife edge of pleasure. She could stay there forever.

Luc bit her neck, ran his tongue over her tightly furled nipples. It was enough. It was too much. She arched her back and gave a choked sob as everything inside her splintered and fanned out through her veins in cascading ripples of pure joy.

Afterward, she was weak as a baby. Luc dried her tenderly and scooped her up in his arms to carry her to their bed. Hattie had lost all sense of time. And didn't really care.

Luc muttered an apology as he slid beneath the covers and moved over her and into her. She had nothing left, but this coupling was warm and lazy. He rode her forever, it seemed, pausing each time he came close to the end and making himself wait, stretching out the incredible connection, the deep, undulating eroticism.

He enveloped her, overwhelmed her. His scent, his touch, his powerful domination.

Somewhere in the deep recesses of her consciousness lingered the knowledge that she would have to pay for this day. That down the line her heart would face pain equal to the present elation.

But she refused to let such maudlin considerations ruin the present.

She put a hand to his cheek, loving him with her eyes. "You're amazing," she whispered. "I haven't felt like this in a very long time."

His cheeks were ruddy, his eyes hooded, his chin shadowed with late-day stubble. Everything about him reeked of uncivilized, ravenous male. Little was left of the suave businessman, the wealthy CEO.

And Hattie loved it…loved him. God help her, she did. This was a man she could live with… share a life with.

But the other Luc still existed outside this room. And that was the problem. Just as it had always been.

He groaned and his whole body shook as his mighty control finally snapped. "Hattie…" He climaxed in a series of long, rapid thrusts.

Despite her exhaustion, echoes of pleasure teased her once again.

In the aftermath, they slept. And as the tropical sun sank low in the sky, coaxing the stars out to play in the gathering dusk, Mr. and Mrs. Luc Cavallo were in perfect accord for one fleeting moment.

Thirteen

Luc rolled over and looked at the clock sometime around 9:00 p.m. His stomach was growling, and no wonder. Their late brunch was the last meal he had eaten.

He slung an arm above his head and yawned, his somber gaze noting that Hattie slept peacefully. Too bad he wasn't as relaxed. The sex had been nothing short of spectacular, but now that his head was in control and not his libido, he was able to think clearly. And the conclusions he drew were unsettling.

He was in danger of falling in love with Hattie all over again. Perhaps in some ways he had never fallen *out* of love…which might explain why the many women he had dated in the last ten years never quite seemed to measure up to some unknown standard. His grandfather had accused him of being too picky…of expecting a paragon of a woman to fill his bed and his life.

Turned out…his grandfather was right.

And that woman was Hattie Parker.

He watched her sleep for a long time, mulling over his options. Right now she needed him because of the baby. Which gave him an advantage for the moment. But what happened when the kid's father was no longer a threat? What then?

Would Hattie try to bid Luc a pleasant goodbye and walk away? The possibility made his chest tight. He was no longer a naive and vulnerable kid. He'd learned his lesson well. Loving someone too much only opened the way for hurt.

Losing both of his parents at the same time had sent him and Leo into a tailspin. Only their grandfather's gruff, tough affection had rescued them. Perhaps way back in college Luc had fallen hard for Hattie because he needed so badly to fill a void in his life.

He was more self-sufficient now, able to enjoy a physical relationship without involving messy emotions. And besides, the barrier between Hattie and him remained the same: his need for control. He had let her too close once upon a time and suffered the consequences. And if his money gave him power, did she expect him to give it all away and live in a shack?

Perhaps since his embarrassment of riches was currently saving her niece, she might decide that being with a wealthy man wasn't exactly a ticket to purgatory.

He touched her arm…he couldn't help himself. The need to keep her close was all-consuming. She had come to him for help…for protection. He would keep Hattie and Deedee safe at all costs. It was the honorable thing to do. And he'd given his word.

Hattie was grateful to him…and she was attracted to him. But that wasn't enough. He wanted her to need him, to depend on him, to beg him to let her stay. How or why she initially came to him didn't really matter in the end. She was vulnerable now. And God help him, he liked it. His course was clear: enjoy the physical side of their marriage as long as it lasted, maintain his emotional distance…and then…

He refused to contemplate the future. Not now when life was close to perfect. He would keep her as long as it suited him.

The next time he awoke, it was morning; dawn to be exact. Clear, liquid light filtered into the bedroom. He stroked his wife's shoulder. She was sleeping on her stomach, her face turned away from him. "Wake up, sleepyhead. I'm starving."

She blinked her eyes and struggled up onto her elbows. One brief glance at her warm, pink breasts was all he got before she rolled onto her back and clutched the sheet to her chest.

Her eyes were wide, her honey-blond hair tousled. "What time is it?"

"Early. We slept through the night. But missing dinner was definitely worth it."

A deep blush painted her face crimson.

He took pity on her. "I'll use the other bathroom to get ready."

"Ready?"

"I thought we'd go snorkeling this morning. Out to the reef. Are you game?"

She frowned. "I've never done it. Is it difficult?"

He patted her leg. "Not really. You'll love it, I

promise." Her expression was unconvinced, so he grinned at her. "Or…we could stay in bed all day."

Hattie stumbled to her feet, almost tripping over her bed-sheet toga. "Snorkeling sounds great," she said, the words breathless as she struggled to maintain her modesty. "If you'll order breakfast, I'll be dressed in a jiff." She disappeared into the bathroom.

He chuckled aloud at her discomfiture. Teasing Hattie had always been fun. Too bad she agreed to the snorkeling. He could have been persuaded to follow option two.

Just thinking about the night before made him hard. With an inward groan, he picked up the phone and called for sustenance. It was going to be a long day, and he needed some serious calories.

Hattie dressed in a modest coral one-piece and covered it with a crisp, white poplin top and khaki walking shorts. A new pair of taupe leather sandals completed the outfit.

When she looked in the mirror, she winced. Going to bed with damp hair meant that she looked like a wild woman. It took a hairbrush and patient determination to tame the mess. Finally, she tucked it up into a ponytail, donned an Atlanta Braves cap and smoothed sheer sunscreen onto her face, neck and arms.

In addition to her new wardrobe, Luc had gifted her with an array of expensive cosmetics. Though most of it was products she would only use for fancy occasions, she had already come to appreciate the many wonderful skin-care creams and lotions.

Breakfast was just arriving when she stepped out of the bathroom. Luc, freshly shaven, his hair damp, tipped the young woman who brought up the largesse.

He spread a hand. "Let's eat."

They consumed an embarrassingly large amount of food in record time. Hattie hadn't realized how hungry she was.

Luc watched her bite into a huge strawberry. "You've got juice all over your chin. Let me..." He dabbed her sticky skin with a cloth napkin, his face close to hers. His expression was shuttered, and she wanted badly to know what he was thinking.

Her head was filled with memories of last night…experiences that were life-changing.

But men were far more cavalier about sex and intimacy. When it was over it was over. Luc might want to be with her again, but that didn't mean he'd be doodling a heart with both their names on scrap paper.

Sex was only physical as far as Luc was concerned. She'd do well to keep that fact firmly planted in the front of her brain. And that meant staying out of this suite as much as possible.

She scooted back from the table. "Let's go. I'm excited about this."

Luc had not chartered a private boat. And for that Hattie was glad. Having other people around diffused the natural awkwardness she was experiencing. She couldn't even look at Luc without remembering how his powerful body had joined with hers, how their skin had been damp with exertion, their muscles lax with pleasure.

If she let herself, she could imagine that they were like any normal newlyweds. Deeply in love, and ravenous for each other.

Luc didn't help her resolve to be sensible. He was in turns tender, affectionate and teasing. More and more she saw glimpses of the young man she had fallen in love with. Away from the pressure of business and responsibilities, Luc laughed often, was more relaxed and carefree.

He handed her a pair of flippers. "Put these on, and I'll help you with your mask." All around them, fellow passengers were doing the same thing. The large catamaran had cut its engines and was bobbing in clear blue-green water over the reef below.

Hattie and Luc had already shed their outer clothing and tucked all of it into a big raffia tote bag. She tried not to drool over her new husband. His black swim trunks were plain, but it was his sculpted torso and powerful arms that drew attention. Hattie didn't miss the fact that she wasn't the only one eyeing Luc's masculine beauty.

He wore expensive, reflective sunglasses that made him look like a movie star. It didn't seem fair for one man to have everything—looks, character and money to burn.

She sighed inwardly as he handed her a mask

and snorkel tube. "What happens if I swallow
water?"

"You'll be fine. I'll be right beside you."

The boat captain gave some basic instructions,
including a warning to listen for the whistle that
signaled time to return to the boat. Hattie was
very glad she had a reliable partner.

She had assumed they would jump over the side
like in the movies, but the catamaran had a ladder
that could be lowered into the water between the
two large hulls. Backing down the steps was a
little claustrophobic, but Luc went first and was
waiting for her as she descended. He took her
arm, his face almost unrecognizable behind his
mask. "Come on, little mermaid. We don't want
to waste any time."

Hattie was not a superconfident swimmer. And
learning to breathe through the tube was chal-
lenging. But Luc's patience and support, along
with a life vest, erased much of her fear, and soon
she was moving through the water, head down,
discovering the wonders of the reef.

The colors were muted and not as dramatic as
Discovery Channel specials she had seen about

the Great Barrier Reef, but the experience was enchanting nevertheless. Corals bobbed and swayed in eerie dances. Multicolored fish, large and small, moved with unconcern in and around the landlubber visitors.

Much of the necessary communication involved pointing and arm touches. But when Hattie spotted a familiar shape, she gasped, swallowed water, and had to come up to catch her breath. "It was a shark," she cried, coughing as she cleared her throat.

Luc shoved his mask on top of his head and laughed. "I've never seen anyone's eyes get that big. I thought you were going to faint dead in the water."

She shuddered. "Don't say dead. I wanted to take some pictures, but he was too fast." The snorkeling package included disposable waterproof cameras. "He wasn't very big though."

Luc tugged her ponytail. "You were hoping for *Jaws?*"

She giggled, feeling happier than she had been in a long time. "Well, not really, but it would have made a great Facebook post."

He glanced at his diver's watch. "We'd better get back to it. Time's almost up."

By the time the whistle sounded, Hattie was ready to quit. The experience was amazing, but the unaccustomed exercise, combined with learning how to manipulate the equipment, had exhausted her.

Back onboard everyone dried off and deposited their gear in large barrels for cleaning. Young crew members passed out lemonade and cookies. Luc and Hattie sat side by side, the wind in their faces as the boat cut rapidly through the waves on the home journey. Their swimsuits dried rapidly in the heat.

Luc put his arm around her back. "Was it what you expected?"

She glanced up at him, controlling a shiver at the delicious feel of his warm skin on hers. "Even better," she said. The sun was making her drowsy. Her head lolled against his shoulder, and she let herself lean into his body.

As they docked in Key West, she roused. It was the work of minutes to slip back into shorts, shoes and top. Luc followed suit, and soon they disembarked with the other passengers.

They lingered at the dock for a few minutes watching parasail enthusiasts go airborne. Hattie shaded her eyes with a hand. "That looks fun, too."

Luc took her arm. "Maybe tomorrow. Let's find a restaurant."

She punched him softly. "Is that all you ever want to do?"

He paused in the middle of the road and kissed her—hard. He brushed a stray hair from her cheek. "Actually, it's way down on the list, but I'm trying to be a considerate husband."

That shut her up. What would Luc say if she demanded to go back to the guesthouse and spend the afternoon and evening as they had the day before?

Sadly, she didn't have the guts to propose what she really wanted to do. Instead, she pretended interest in the fried plantains at the Cuban restaurant they found near the harbor. She ate mechanically. Every moment that passed brought them closer to the evening hours. When they would go to bed…together?

The uncertainty made her crazy. Was last night a one-time faux pas on their parts, or was Luc assuming they would continue to have sex for the duration of the marriage?

Hattie hated the idea of divorce, but what choice did they have? They had allowed sexual hunger and curiosity to lead them down a dangerous path, and she knew what happened to that proverbial cat.

Luc nudged her elbow. "I thought you'd be hungry. Swimming always gives me an appetite."

She shrugged. "I think it's the heat getting to me. Do you mind if we go back to our place? I'd love to take a shower and wash the seawater off my skin."

His fork stilled in midair, and his cheekbones went dark. He cleared his throat. "Of course. Whatever you want."

Hattie cursed her own artless stupidity. Did that sound like an open invitation for sex? She hadn't meant it that way.

Or had she?

Luc finished his meal and summoned the waiter for their check. Shortly after, they made their way through the crowded streets. Apparently, many tourists had arrived early to celebrate the Memorial Day holiday. Hattie barely noticed the commotion. All she could think about was how to handle the return to their luxurious bridal quarters.

The leather seats in the car were hot…no shade trees this time. She wriggled uncomfortably, and rolled down her window to let the steamy air escape. Luc was silent, his face impossible to read.

The ride was brief and silent. They exited the car. Marcel welcomed them as they strolled through the courtyard. "Are you enjoying your stay in Key West?"

Luc shook his hand, but Hattie answered. "It's lovely. So vibrant and colorful. You're lucky to live here year-round."

Marcel nodded as he trimmed an overgrown bougainvillea. "The only time I rethink my address is during hurricane season, but we are lucky here in the Keys…very few major hits."

Luc frowned. "Have you heard a forecast for tonight and tomorrow?"

"Nothing but calm, clear skies. Perfect vacation weather."

Hattie preceded Luc up the stairs, wondering what was up. Luc seemed focused on some unknown objective. And once in their room, instead of throwing her on the bed as she had hoped or expected, he seemed to be preoccupied...or at least avoiding sex at the moment. "Why were you concerned about the weather?" she asked him.

He tossed the car keys and his sunglasses on the dresser. "I have an idea."

"Uh-oh," she teased. "Should I be worried?"

He sprawled on the sofa. "Do you remember those camping trips we took in college?"

"Of course." They had journeyed to the north Georgia mountains a number of times, spending several chilly spring and autumn nights curled together in a double sleeping bag...just the two of them. Those had been magical times, and Hattie had loved them even more because the outings were inexpensive.

His arms stretched along the back of the couch, his fingers drumming restlessly. "I thought it might be fun to do that again."

In this heat? Was Luc so spooked by the intense emotion of the night before that he was going to keep them busy, nonstop? "Umm, well..."

"There's an island with an old fort. We can

camp there. It would be an adventure. What do you say?"

The boyish eagerness on his face was irresistible. Despite her better judgment, she managed an enthusiastic smile. "Sounds like fun."

Fourteen

While Luc was on the phone making arrangements for their impromptu trip, Hattie showered
and then checked in with Ana.

The baby is fine. No problem. Enjoy yourselves.

Hattie ended her call and surveyed the room.
Luc was paying who knew how much money for
this wonderful suite, and yet he wanted to abandon it for parts unknown. Men...She found him
in the sitting room, still on the phone, but now
she could tell it was business. Knowing what she
did of his work ethic and his drive and determination, it really surprised her that he had been
willing and able to get away for a honeymoon,
pretend or otherwise.

He hung up and turned to face her, jubilation on his face. "I got us two spots. They only allow a small number of campers each night. But there's one catch."

"Oh?"

He winced, gauging her reaction. "We have to leave right now."

"Seriously?"

"Yeah. Everything for the week was full except for tonight."

Gulp. "Okay. What do I need to pack?"

"Anything that's comfortable and cool. Plus a swimsuit. We'll be able to snorkel in the shallow water around the fort."

And at night? What would happen then?

Hattie pondered that question. And how did one prepare for possible seduction on a remote, uninhabited island? After dithering in the bedroom for several minutes, she dumped out her carry-on bag and began filling it methodically. One set of clean clothes and underwear. Swimsuit. A long T-shirt to sleep in. Sunscreen.

She picked up a lilac silk nightgown and held it to her cheek for a wistful moment. Not exactly camping attire. But what the heck. This was her honeymoon. She stuffed it in.

It was easy to see why Luc was so successful. In barely an hour, he had secured bags of food, all sorts of camping gear, two coolers and transportation. They found parking near the dock and unloaded. Hattie was stunned to see Luc walk toward a stylish, powerful speedboat.

He held out a hand. "Come aboard, my lady."

The vessel must have been wickedly expensive, even as a rental. Everything about it gleamed, from the hardwood deck to the shiny chrome trim. Luc stowed their supplies and tossed Hattie a yellow life jacket.

She wrinkled her nose. "Do I have to?"

He slid his arms into a navy one. "Captain's orders."

"How far are we going?"

"About seventy miles."

Her apprehension must have shown on her face, because he sobered. "It's perfectly safe, Hattie. Leo and I learned to pilot boats before we could drive cars. Grandfather's villa is on the shores of Lake Como, and as teenage boys, we spent all the time we could in and on the water. I'll take care of you, I promise."

He was as good as his word, and in his competent hands, the sleek craft ate up the miles effortlessly. Hattie had donned her baseball cap back at the dock, and she was glad, because the wind whipped and slapped them in joyous abandon.

At times, dolphins leaped beside the boat, gamboling playfully, their beautiful skin glistening in the sun. Hattie laughed in delight and sat back finally, her eyes closed, her face tilted toward the sun. If she and Luc could keep going forever into the next sunset, life would be perfect.

Or almost. She couldn't bear the thought of giving up her niece. Deedee wasn't a burden. The baby was a joy.

Hattie shook off reality with a deliberate toss of her head. She took advantage of Luc's concentration to watch him unobserved. He controlled the boat with a relaxed stance that gave testament to his comfort being on the water. When several dark shapes began growing ahead of them, she scooted up beside him. "Is that it?"

He gave her a sideways grin. "Yep. We're in Dry Tortugas National Park."

"Never heard of it."

"Well it's only been a national park since 1992, so that's not so surprising."

"Why the name?"

"*Tortugas* because they look like a group of turtles, and *Dry* because there's no fresh water on any of them."

As they neared their destination, she stared, incredulous. She and Luc were miles from civilization, literally in the middle of nowhere. Yet perched on a handkerchief-size piece of land sat a sturdy brick fort, its hexagonal walls enclosing a large grassy area, and its perimeter surrounded by a water-filled moat. Even at a distance, the evidence of crumbling decay was visible.

Luc waved a hand as he throttled back the engine. "Fort Jefferson."

Hattie leaned her hands on the railing and absorbed it all. "I can't believe this."

"You know the expression 'Your name is mud'?"

She nodded as Luc tied up to the dock. "Of course."

"Some people attribute that remark to Dr.

Samuel Mudd who was incarcerated here in the 1860s."

"What did he do that was so terrible?"

"He had the misfortune to set the broken leg of John Wilkes Booth after Booth assassinated President Lincoln."

"Wow."

"Exactly. Mudd was convicted of treason and sent here to serve a life sentence."

Hattie shuddered. Knowing there was no possibility of escape must have been mentally anguishing. "How dreadful."

"The story does have a bit of a happy ending," Luc said. "As you can imagine, disease was rampant in the fort. Dysentery, malaria, smallpox… and, at one time, a terrible outbreak of yellow fever. It was so bad, the entire medical staff died."

"And that's where Dr. Mudd comes to the rescue?"

"Right. Even knowing as he did that the disease was a killer, he stepped in and began caring for the soldiers, saving dozens of lives. For his heroism, he ultimately received a full pardon and was allowed to return home."

Hattie pondered the sad story. She wasn't a

superstitious person, but the island, beautiful though it was, carried an aura of past suffering. Dr. Mudd had earned a second chance. Would Hattie and Luc be as lucky?

Luc had arranged for one of the park ranger's sons to unload all their supplies and set up camp. Luc lent a hand, but even so, it took several loads to carry everything to the designated camping area, a small sandy strip of land lightly dotted with grass and shrubs. At the far end, a young family with two kids had already erected a red-and-white tent.

Luc handled the minimal paperwork with the ranger on duty and then turned to Hattie. "You ready for a swim?"

Disappointment colored her words. "I thought we were going to explore the fort."

He held up his hands and laughed. "Okay. Fine. Maybe it will be a little cooler in there."

They grabbed cameras and water bottles and headed out. The empty silent rooms in the fort almost reeked of despair. The thick walls blocked out some of the afternoon heat, but at the same time contributed to the oppressive dungeonlike atmosphere. There were no furnishings. The stark, barren chambers seemed to echo with the voices of long-ago inmates.

After wandering through several sections of the fort, Luc pointed out the entrance to Dr. Mudd's cell. Hattie read aloud the inscription over the arch. *"Whoso entereth here leaveth all hopes behind."* She shuddered. "Gruesome. But it sounds familiar."

Luc nodded. "It's from Dante's *Inferno*."

"I need to see the sky," she muttered. She stepped back out into the sunshine, noting again the way the bricks were slowly disintegrating as time took its toll. "Can we climb the lighthouse?"

Luc took her arm. "It's about a thousand degrees today. The lighthouse is inactive. And I need a swim."

"Wimp," she teased. But she allowed herself to be persuaded. Back at the tent, there was an awkward moment.

Luc avoided her gaze. "Not much room in there," he said gruffly. "You go first."

It didn't take her long. Later, while she waited for Luc to change, she shaded her eyes and watched the numerous boats anchored offshore. Divers were taking advantage of the opportunity to explore the reef and other items of interest on the ocean floor.

When Luc emerged from the tent, she swallowed. He was wearing black nylon racing trunks that left little to the imagination. She smiled weakly, her temples perspiring, as he tossed her a towel.

Luc slung an arm around her shoulders, his own towel around his neck. "Let's go."

The water felt blissfully cool. Hattie paddled happily in the shallow water near the fort, finding it a lot easier than her first experience, since she could occasionally stand up. Some of the boaters were snorkeling as well, but they stayed mostly to the back of the fort.

She noticed that the family with the two children was also taking advantage of an afternoon swim. It suddenly occurred to her to wonder how far sound carried on the night air. Her breathing hitched, and she shivered despite the blazing sun. Anticipation and anxiety mingled in her stomach, making her feel slightly faint. If she got in over her head tonight, she'd have no one to blame but herself.

Luc had been swimming in deeper water, but

he reappeared suddenly by her side, tugging off his mask and running a hand through his hair, flinging drops of water everywhere.

He smiled lazily. "Having fun?"

She nodded. "It's amazing."

He glanced at his high tech waterproof watch. "I thought I'd go on back and set up the grill, get the fire started. Will you be okay?"

She motioned him away. "By all means. I'm working up an appetite."

Without warning, he lifted her against his wet chest, her feet dangling in the water. His head lowered. "So am I, Hattie. So am I."

His mouth found hers, and the raw sensuality of his kiss made her dizzy. She closed her eyes, her other senses intensifying. He tasted salty, with a hint of coconut from the sunscreen he'd used. She pulled his lower lip between her teeth and bit gently.

His entire body quaked. He released her slowly, allowing her to slide the length of his virtually nude form. By the time her feet touched the sandy bottom once again, she could barely stand.

He laughed shakily. "Well, hell. I don't know if I have the strength to climb out of the water." He rested his chin on the top of her head, his arms wrapped around her waist. "You know what's going to happen tonight."

She nodded, mute, her face pressed to the muscular flesh just above his nipple.

He released her and stepped back. "Okay, then."

An hour later, they ate dinner in style. Hattie should have known that a Cavallo wouldn't prepare anything as plebian as hamburgers or hot dogs. Luc grilled T-bones and fresh shrimp over mesquite charcoal and then produced corn on the cob and potato salad to go with it.

She looked at him wryly over her heaping plate. "This isn't how I remember camping."

He shrugged. "My tastes have matured."

They lingered over their al fresco meal. Hattie was relaxed and yet keenly aware of the tension humming between them. Luc offered fresh chocolate-dipped strawberries for dessert. She bit into one carefully, licking the sweet juice from her lower lip.

He watched her constantly until she swatted his arm. "Stop it."

His wide, rakish grin was all innocence. "I don't know what you mean."

Moments later, the teenager showed up to do
KP. He would be leaving soon when his father
went off duty. There was no official presence at
the fort overnight.

Luc suggested a boat ride. The sun was beginning its slow decline. Hattie prepared her camera.
Luc steered the boat to a perfect vantage point
to get shots of the fort washed in the beautiful
evening light.

Afterward they anchored in deep water and
dropped the ladder over the side. Hattie climbed
over the rail, but Luc made a neat dive off the
rear of the boat.

They swam and played for a long time, until
the light began to fade. Back on the boat, they
dried off and Hattie put on a T-shirt over her suit.
As they picked up speed, the stiff breeze raised
goose bumps on her arms and legs.

While they were tying up once again at the boat
dock, the young father from the family across the
way approached them.

He shook Luc's hand and smiled ruefully. "Our
youngest son has developed an earache, and
we know from past experience that we'll need
medicine, so we're going back to Key West. We

wanted to tell someone, because the park service occasionally does a head count out here."

Luc grimaced. "That's too bad. It's going to be a beautiful night. But I'll help you load up."

Hattie walked back to the tent and stretched out on a sleeping bag. Daylight was fading fast. It was a half hour before Luc returned. Out the tent flap she could see the family pull away from the dock. The other boats she had watched offshore earlier in the day had long since lifted anchor and sailed or motored away.

For the first time since their arrival, she and Luc were completely, irrevocably alone.

He crouched and held out a hand. "Let's take a walk."

While she stretched her arms over her head and then donned a windbreaker, Luc retrieved a flashlight from his pack and zipped up the tent. They approached the fort and skirted the edge until they could step onto the sea wall. For most of the perimeter of the fort, the barrier separated the moat from the sea.

Hattie didn't need Luc's warning to watch her step. Although the wall wasn't particularly narrow, the thought of falling into the mysterious ocean was daunting.

On the far side of the fort they sat down, cross-legged, and surveyed the vast expanse of sky and sea. A tiny sliver of new moon did little to illuminate the night. As their eyes became accustomed to the dark, they could just make out the faint line of demarcation separating the silvery pewter of the ocean from the midnight-blue of the sky. Several miles away, a working lighthouse flashed a periodic caution to boats, warning of the reefs and small rocky islands.

They sat in silence for several minutes. Hattie finally whispered, "It's like we're the only two people in the entire world. I'm not sure I like the feeling."

He took her hand and squeezed it. "Do you want to go back?"

"No." She leaned her head on his shoulder. "It's beautiful and awe-inspiring, and a little frightening to be honest, but I wouldn't have missed this for anything. Can you imagine what it must be like here during a hurricane?"

Luc chuckled. "I don't even want to think about it."

They sat hand in hand for a long time, wrapped

in a cocoon of darkness and the intimacy of complete isolation. Far out across the waves, traces of phosphorescence lent a ghostly aura to the night.

Eventually, by unspoken consent, they made their way back around to the campsite. After a quick visit to the Spartan toilet facilities near the dock, they met back at the tent and stood facing each other.

Luc lifted a hand and traced her chin with his thumb. "It's not too late to change your mind. We have a perfectly good king-size bed back at the hotel. I can wait if you'd rather."

She took a step closer, leaning into his chest. "I want you, Luc…tonight."

Fifteen

She felt his chest lift and fall as a shuddering breath escaped his lungs. He wrapped his arms around her. "Do you need a few minutes in the tent to get ready?"

"Yes," she muttered, her throat tight with nervousness. He handed her the small flashlight. She unzipped the tent and knelt to climb in, carefully removing her shoes and leaving them in a corner so no sand would find its way into their comfy sleeping space.

Luc had spread thick, soft sleeping bags on top of a single, large, cushiony air mattress. Since it was too hot to sleep inside the bags, he had also procured crisp cotton sheets complete with small pillows tucked inside lace-edged cases. The resulting effect was one part *Out of Africa* and two parts *Pretty Woman,* a stage unmistakably set for seduction.

Earlier, Hattie had regarded the tent as pleasantly roomy. Now, with Luc standing somewhere outside, it felt surprisingly claustrophobic, especially when she imagined Luc's large frame dominating the enclosed space.

She picked up her overnight case and found her toiletry bag. After quickly cleaning her face, she stripped off her clothes, thankful that the evening swim had left her skin feeling cool, if a bit salty. Luc had thought to bring a small container of fresh water, so she dampened a cloth and used it to further freshen up.

At Luc's murmured request, she passed the water container and a clean towel out to him. While he was presumably taking care of his ablutions, she found a tube of scented lotion and applied it to her elbows and legs and one or two other interesting spots.

She pulled out the lilac gown and slipped it over her head, relishing the feel of the silk against her bare skin. When she was done, she tucked the flashlight under Luc's pillow, leaving only the smallest beam of light to illuminate the tent.

Taking a deep breath and smoothing her hair, she called out. "I'm ready."

The tent flap peeled back instantly, and she saw him place his shoes and the water canister inside at the foot of the tent before he crawled in, immediately dwarfing the tiny space. He had already undressed.

Hattie's heart stopped for a split second, and then lurched back into service with an unsteady beat. Even her ploy with the flashlight didn't disguise his impressive attributes. She put a hand against her breastbone, feeling a bit like a Regency virgin in need of smelling salts.

Luc zipped the tent flap shut, tossed a few foil packets beside his pillow, and then stretched out with a sigh onto the comfortable bedding. He lay on his side facing her, leaning on his elbow with one leg propped up, looking like a centerfold.

Only, he was real. Here. In the flesh.

Hattie remained seated, her spine stiff as a poker, her legs paralyzed in a pretzel position. He patted the space beside him, and she saw him smile. "You're too far away," he complained.

She uncurled her legs and scooted closer, still leaving a healthy distance between them.

He reached out and smoothed a hand over her thigh covered in lilac silk. "I'm betting you didn't order this little number from L.L. Bean," he said, the words laced with amusement.

Suddenly, he reached behind him and picked up the flashlight, momentarily blinding her when he pointed it in her direction. He focused the tiny beam of light on her left shoulder.

His voice came out of the darkness. "Ditch the gown, Hattie, starting with that strap."

She couldn't see his face, only the outline of his body. Her fingers went to the slim strap he'd indicated, and she lowered it, slipping her arm free, but keeping her breast covered.

The beam of light moved to her other shoulder. "Now that one."

The second strap fell. She put a hand against her chest to hold the gown in place.

The light slipped down to her abdomen. He spoke again, his tone hoarse and rough. "Now all of it."

She rose to her knees, trembling, and let the fabric fall to her hips, and then, with a little shimmy, to the sleeping bag. Luc's indrawn breath was audible. The beam of light rose slowly to circle one breast and then the other. Her nipples tightened painfully. The light slid over the taut plane of her stomach to rest in the shadowed valley between her thighs.

His voice this time was barely a whisper. "Hand me the gown."

She lifted her knees, an awkward maneuver given the situation, and pulled the silk free, tossing it to him.

He buried his face in the cloth momentarily. Then the light went out. He called her name. "Hattie…come here."

She tumbled forward, her eagerness assisted by his firm grasp on her forearm. She landed half-sprawled across his chest, and one of her hands lodged in an interesting position between his legs. She found the hot, smooth length of him and stroked gently.

Luc groaned, covering her lips with his, the kiss ravenous and demanding. His tongue plundered the recesses of her mouth, exploring every crevice, nibbling and biting until she was breathless and whimpering with need.

Seconds later she sensed him trying to slow things down, but it was too late. While he fumbled for a condom, she rubbed her breasts against his chest, savoring the delicious friction. She felt his hands settle on her bottom. He lifted her until she sat astride him, and she tensed.

On and off during the last decade she had dreamed about being with him. But those fleeting fantasies didn't come close to approximating the reality of Luc Cavallo, naked, nudging with barely concealed impatience at the heart of her feminine passage.

She arched her back and felt him enter her, stretching her to an almost painful fullness. "Oh, Luc…" The sensation was incredible.

He froze, not moving an inch, his body taut and trembling. "Am I hurting you?"

She choked out a laugh, wriggling, forcing him centimeters deeper. "No." It was all she could manage. She raked his nipples with her fingernails. He heaved beneath her, burying himself to the hilt. The connection was stunning—her, adjusting to the sensation of his possession, him, clearly struggling for control.

He lifted his hands to cup her sensitive breasts.

She cried out, nearing a peak so intense, she could feel it hovering just out of reach. He withdrew almost completely, but before she could voice a protest, he thrust even deeper, initiating a rhythm that sent them both tumbling into a fiery release. Somewhere in the fringes of her consciousness, she heard him shout as he emptied himself into her body, but her orgasm washed over her with such power, she was unable to focus on anything but her own pleasure.

Luc lay perfectly still, trying to recover from the effects of Hurricane Hattie. Her slender body lay draped over his in sensual abandon that filled him with a fierce masculine satisfaction overlaid by the terrifying realization that he had fallen in love with her...again. Far away from the familiar trappings of his daily life, it was all so clear. He didn't need *things* to be happy...not money or electronic toys or even the adrenaline-producing challenge of his job.

His arms tightened around her. A time machine couldn't have taken him back any more successfully than this sham marriage and this ill-conceived honeymoon. Hattie filled his life with an exhilaration he had experienced only once before. She brought *fun* into his days, joy into his home, passion into his bed.

But nothing had changed. He was still rich, and she was still wary about ceding power and control to a man like him.

The baby was the fragile glue holding this house of cards together. Unless he could convince Hattie that great sex covered a multitude of sins, it was only a matter of time until she left him.

He sighed as he felt her tongue trace his collarbone. The slightly rough caress sent trickles of heat down his torso straight to his groin. He smoothed his fingers over her bottom, guiltily aware that he might have bruised her pale skin.

She leaned on her elbow and kissed him briefly. "I think I've developed a whole new appreciation for roughing it…if I can say that with a straight face while lying on 800 thread count sheets."

He chuckled. "I never knew you liked it rough."

She punched his arm. "You're so bad. But I like that about you…" Her head found its way to his shoulder.

As her voice trailed off, he shifted her to one side. Not that he didn't enjoy having her body glued to his like wallpaper, but her proximity made it difficult to form a coherent thought. He hoped that if he handled this interlude correctly, he might be able to bind Hattie to him in such a way that she couldn't escape.

Women, unlike most men, had a hard time separating sex from emotional ties. All he had to do was convince Hattie that the compatibility they experienced in bed could carry over to life in general. That the incredible sex was only a sign of their overall rightness for each other… that they had more in common than she realized.

When Hattie slipped a hand across his thigh, he lost all interest in thinking. Her curious fingers found his partially erect shaft and began exploring. He shuddered, giving himself up to the heady pleasure of having Hattie map his body with an eagerness that was as flattering as it was arousing.

Her questing hands feathered over him like butterfly wings, brushing, touching. He clenched his teeth against a surge of lust as she found a particularly sensitive spot. "Hattie…"

She nipped his hipbone with her teeth. "Hmmm?"

His hands tangled in her hair, and he pulled her up for a hard kiss. This time, it was her tongue that demanded entrance, taunting his mouth with sweet little licks and strokes that made him groan with hunger.

Almost…almost he lifted her astride him as he had earlier, craving the sensation of filling her with one swift thrust. But at the last second, he broke the kiss and pushed her to her back, determined this time to give her the tenderness and attention she deserved.

She reached for him, but he eluded her, sliding down the length of her body to concentrate on the source of her pleasure. His hands glided over her skin, skin softer than any silk nightgown. He traced her navel and abdomen with his tongue. She twisted restlessly.

Gripping her hips and holding her down, he bent his head lower, ignoring her incoherent protests. She stiffened at the first touch of his lips, her back arching off the sleeping bag. A panting cry escaped her. He licked gently, and seconds later she shattered in a moaning climax.

He scooped her into his arms, holding her tightly as the last tremors racked her body. She was his. He was familiar with sexual satisfaction, but this need to claim, to possess, was something he had experienced only one other time in his life.

When she stirred in his embrace, he stroked the hair from her face with an unsteady hand. He kissed her softly, tenderly, trying to tell her with his touch what he knew she wasn't ready to hear in words.

The kiss lengthened. Deepened. His own unappeased arousal clawed to the surface, reminding him that making Hattie fly moments ago was only a prelude. He rose over her, trapping both her hands in one of his and raising them above her head. His maneuver lifted her breasts in silent invitation. With his free hand, he caressed them, stroking the petal-soft curves, avoiding her nipples, deliberately building her need once again.

When her pleading whispers and writhing hips told him she was ready for his possession, he abandoned her breasts and slid his hand between her legs, testing her heat and dampness with one finger.

She turned her head and bit the tender flesh of his inner arm, silently demanding. He released her hands, scarcely noticing when they grasped his shoulders. His need had become a roaring torrent, a driving urgency toward completion. Damning the necessity, he sheathed his rock-hard erection in a condom.

With one knee, he spread her legs and settled between her thighs, positioning himself. He looked down at her, inwardly cursing the darkness, needing desperately to see her face. "Tell me you want me, Hattie," he said huskily. "Beg me."

She spread her legs even wider, seeking to join their bodies, but he held back, driven by some Neanderthal impulse. "Say it, Hattie."

Her voice, a rasping, air-starved whisper reached his ear. "Please Luc. Take me…please."

He surged forward, shuddering as her body gripped him. She was tight and hot, and her long, slender legs wrapped around his waist. He knew in an instant that once more there would be no slow, sweet loving. He drove into her again and again until the tide swept over him, pulled him under, erasing every thought but one. Hattie was his.

He tried to hold back, to prolong the exquisite

sensations for a few moments more, but it was hopeless. With a hoarse shout, he came inside her for long, agonizing seconds, conscious of nothing but searing pleasure and blinding release.

In the aftermath, they clung together, breathing fractured, skin damp, hearts pounding in unison. With his last ounce of energy, he reached for the top sheet, pulled it over them. Hattie's limp body curled spoon fashion against his, her bare bottom pressed to the cradle of his thighs.

Luc surrendered to the oblivion of sleep.

Sixteen

Hattie slipped from Luc's arms and donned a long T-shirt and panties before quietly exiting the tent. Her body was stiff and sore in some interesting places, and she felt at once exhausted and exhilarated.

After a necessary trip to the bathroom, she stood in the eerie gray light of predawn, her arms clasped around her middle. Just a few hundred feet offshore, a tiny strip of land, hardly big enough to merit the designation *island,* was covered with a teeming mass of flapping, squawking birds.

Their raucous calls and noisy confusion mirrored the turmoil in her heart. What in the heck was she going to do? There was no longer any doubt about her feelings for Luc. Having sex with him last night in such an erotic and abandoned way had been at once the most perfect and the most stupid thing she had ever done in her life.

She might one day find another man as intelligent as Luc. As kind, as handsome, as funny... perhaps. But there was no doubt in her mind that the lovemaking they had shared was unique. He'd been a good lover in college, no question. But this time around, the sex was even better. She hadn't expected the intensity, the shattering intimacy, the feeling that she had bound herself to him body and soul.

He was also better at reading her. Some internal radar seemed to pick up her moods, to see inside her head and know what she was thinking. Which made him very dangerous to her peace of mind.

And his empathy was a huge problem given that this relationship was temporary and supposedly pragmatic. She didn't want to feel so connected to him. What a mess. As much as she longed to enjoy this surprising honeymoon all the way to its conclusion, another smarter Hattie said, *Go home.*

She looked over her shoulder at the small blue tent, its outline shrouded in the misty morning fog. In a short while, the cozy housing would be dismantled, much like her short-lived marriage. The campsite would be cleared, leaving no trace of the spot where Hattie Parker had given her heart to Luc Cavallo.

But hearts healed, didn't they? And life went on. She would go back to her job perhaps, settle into a new place, learn to play the role of single mom. And perhaps this ending wouldn't be as painful as the one ten years ago. Maybe Deedee's chortling smiles would be a distraction.

Hattie and Luc might remain friends…or, if not, she'd have memories.… And if she was lucky, someday a lover who didn't know that he was second best.

Luc knew the instant Hattie stirred from his embrace and left the tent. Even in his sleep he'd been aware of her warmth and softness twined in his arms, their legs tangled, her head tucked beneath his chin. Twice more during the night they had come together in exquisite lovemaking, the first a slow gentle mating, the second a hard, fast, almost desperate race to the finish.

But Hattie's recent stealthy departure said louder than words that she needed some time alone. That she hadn't wanted to face him. He understood her motivation. He just didn't like it.

The warm pillows still retained a remnant of her fragrance. He climbed out and put on his shorts. As he ran a hand over the stubble on his chin, he grimaced. Perhaps spending the night on a deserted island wasn't the greatest way to win over a woman. But Hattie had been a good sport about it all, and something about the isolation had deepened the intimacy of their lovemaking.

He exited the tent and walked over to where she stood looking out to sea. Looping his arms around her waist from behind, he rested his chin on the top of her head. "Good morning."

She turned slightly, enough for him to see that she was smiling. "Good morning, Luc."

He squeezed her gently. "You ready for some breakfast?"

She nodded. "At the risk of sounding unlady-like, I could eat the proverbial horse."

They fixed the meal together, Hattie cutting up fresh fruit while he toasted bread on the grill. He had hoped to make love to her once more before they left, but it wasn't going to happen. Hattie had retreated to some distant place, and the invisible line in the sand was one he couldn't cross.

By ten o'clock everything was packed up and loaded in the boat. He suggested climbing the lighthouse, but Hattie shook her head, saying she was tired and ready to go back. He wanted to tease her about her fatigue. Lord knew neither of them had gotten much sleep, but his courage failed him. He had just experienced one of the most incredible nights of his life, but the lady involved was treating him like a favorite brother.

It was hell on a man's self-esteem.

They made the return trip to Key West mostly in silence. Hattie sat in the back of the boat on a bench seat wearing her baseball cap pulled low over her eyes and with her arms curled around her knees. Clouds had rolled in during the morning, making the sky sullen and angry. He had to keep both hands on the wheel to handle the choppy waves.

Docking, unloading and getting back to the

hotel were interminable chores. He was determined to have his say, strangely afraid that if he
didn't mend some unknown rift, she would slip
away from him altogether.

Hattie unlocked the door to their room. He followed her in. She dumped her things on the sofa
and turned to face him, a forced smile on her
lips. "Thanks for taking me to the fort. It was
wonderful."

His jaw clenched. "And what about us? Were
we wonderful, too?"

He watched as shock followed by what could
only be described as a flash of pain crossed her
face.

As she took off her cap and ran her hands
through her hair, she glanced at him. "What do
you think?"

He jammed his hands in his pockets to keep
from reaching for her. "I think we were pretty
damn fabulous.... Wouldn't you agree?"

A rosy flush climbed from her throat to her
cheeks. She nodded slowly. "We never had trouble in that department."

He laughed softly. "Hell, no." He sensed a soft-
ening in her, so he pressed his advantage. "Imag-

ine what we could do in that big bed with wine and clean sheets and candles."

Her blush deepened. He stepped toward her, smiling inwardly as she backed up until her legs hit the sofa and she fell backward. He leaned over her, bracing his hands on the back of the couch, bracketing her with his arms. "Kiss me, Hattie."

Her dark eyes looking up at him were filled with secrets. "Do you really think we'll stop with a kiss?"

He bent to nuzzle her neck. "Does it matter?"

"We're both pretty grungy." She twisted her lips. "I could use a shower."

He nibbled the skin behind her ear, coming down beside her and scooping her into his lap. "I hadn't noticed."

She sighed as he kissed his way around to her collarbone, pushing aside the neckline of her T-shirt to gain easier access. He slid a hand beneath the hem and stroked her breast through her bra, lightly pinching the nipple. She groaned. "Luc…"

The flush on her cheeks deepened when he slipped a hand inside her shorts, finding the soft fluff between her legs. She arched into his caress, her breathing ragged.

He'd been teasing earlier. He had every intention of giving her a quick kiss and then getting some business done while she was in the shower. But Hattie was smarter than he was. Clearly a kiss wasn't enough.

He ripped at the zipper on her shorts, jerking it down and removing those and her panties in one quick maneuver. Seconds later, he had her beneath him as he settled between her legs. Hearing her chant his name in soft whispers went straight to his gut. Somewhere deep in the recesses of his brain he realized this was dangerous. This mindless, desperate urge to take her. But he couldn't stop. Didn't want to.

He entered her a bare inch and hesitated, his body racked with tremors. Her eyes fluttered shut. He touched her cheek. "Look at me, Hattie."

She complied, her eyes cloudy and unfocused. He went an inch deeper, and they groaned in unison. She panted, her chest rising and falling rapidly, but she held his gaze.

Struggling for almost nonexistent control, he

stroked her cheekbone. "We have to deal with this."

Her head moved slowly in a gesture that could have been agreement or denial. "You talk too much." She grabbed a handful of his hair, pulling his head down for a kiss. "Just get on with it."

The breathless demand snapped his feeble efforts to maintain any kind of sanity. If she wanted it, he'd give it to her. No questions asked. He drove deeper into the hot, tight warmth of her, wanting desperately to make it last longer, but realizing with a sort of incredulous despair that he was losing the battle.

He gritted his teeth, holding back the scalding rush of pleasure. But Hattie's sudden cry and his own body defeated him. He surged harder, blindly emptying himself until he felt blackness close in around him.

A long time later he rolled off of her and flopped onto his back on the plush carpet, staring at the ceiling fan rotating overhead. He felt Hattie's fingers twine with his, and heard her voice, filled with unmistakable amusement. "Now I *really* need a shower."

He laughed, stung by chagrin at his emotionally reckless behavior but filled with a deep, boneless contentment. He glanced at his watch and swore. "I have to make two quick calls. But I won't be long, I promise."

She leaned over to kiss him. "It's okay, Luc. Really."

"And was it okay that I took you like a wild man?"

"You *were* pretty intense."

Remorse rode him for not even fully undressing her. "What can I say? You're a temptress."

She looked down at her rumpled clothes and rolled her eyes. "Oh, yeah…that's it."

He stood up, and she followed suit as they each adjusted their clothing. Though he wanted nothing more than to drag her into the bedroom, he resisted the urge. Unless he knew for sure that Hattie was falling for him, he'd be well-advised to rein in his sexual enthusiasm.

But he couldn't resist the urge to woo her. "Why don't we go somewhere fancy for dinner? We can talk about your situation, maybe dance a little…"

Her expression was difficult to read. "That would be nice."

"And we can relax by the pool this afternoon. I'll get Marcel to serve us lunch out there."

"Sure."

He watched her turn toward the bedroom. "I could join you in the shower," he said, consigning his phone calls to the devil.

Hattie shook her head. "Do what you have to do. We've got plenty of time."

Luc let her go for the moment. She was his, body and soul. Perhaps she didn't know it yet, but he would fight dirty if he had to. He wouldn't lose her.… Not again.

Hattie stepped under the strong, stinging spray of the shower and luxuriated in the hot, steamy flow of water. It was amazing what twenty-four hours of deprivation could accomplish. She would never have made it on that TV survivor show. Never mind eating bugs; she would have begged to be voted off after the second day just so she could be clean again.

She dried off with one of the inn's sinfully thick towels. A nap sounded appealing, but she wasn't prepared to give up a day of sunbathing. Donning a robe, she returned to the bedroom and rummaged in her suitcase for the only swimsuit she had not yet worn. It wasn't at all skimpy by today's standards, but the shiny gold fabric clung to her body like a second skin. When Luc appeared in the doorway, his jaw actually dropped. "Tell me you're not wearing that thing outside our room."

She grinned, and then summoned a pout. "I thought you would love it."

He strode toward her. "Love it, hell. When a suit looks like that on a woman, the designer's only motivation is to drive men insane." He skimmed his hands over her body. "Good Lord. It feels like you're naked." He smoothed her bottom. "Are you sure you want to go to the pool? It's nice and quiet and cool up here in our room."

Though the coaxing note in his voice made her knees weak, Hattie held him at arm's length. "I want to go home with at least a semblance of a tan. So I refuse to be distracted by your masculine charms."

He lifted an eyebrow. "You think I'm charming?"

"I think I've made that pretty obvious this week."

He laughed, and for a brief second, she wondered if he felt anything more for her than lust. His actions seemed to indicate affection, but nothing he had said in any context contradicted his earlier plan to make their marriage temporary.

She wanted so badly to say the words swelling in her heart, but she chickened out. It was still too soon.

When Luc's cell phone rang she headed for the door. "You get that if you want to. I'll be out at the pool."

The concern in his words when he spoke with the caller stopped Hattie dead in her tracks.

The conversation was brief. Luc hung up, his expression serious.

Her skin chilled. "What's wrong?"

"The baby's running a temperature."

Hattie sank onto the sofa. "How bad?"

"A hundred and three. It's probably just a virus. They're on the way to a pediatrician right now. Ana wasn't unduly concerned, but she was sure you'd want to know."

"I do. Of course."

Luc eyed her. "What are you thinking?"

She winced, feeling ungrateful for all he had done. "Do you mind if we go home? I need to be with her…to make sure she's okay."

He nodded. "I thought as much. Start packing, and I'll see what kind of flights I can find."

Seventeen

It was almost midnight when they made it back to Atlanta and drove from the airport to the house. Leo was on hand to pick them up since they didn't have a car. He and Luc sat in the front. Hattie in the back.

Leo looked over his shoulder. "How was Key West?"

"Very nice," she replied, refusing to be baited.

The two brothers chuckled in unison. Hattie pretended a sudden interest in the passing scenery.

Leo helped unload the luggage into the foyer, shook Luc's hand and kissed Hattie on the cheek.

"Let me know how Deedee is. I'll be at the office in the morning."

As he drove off, Hattie yawned. Ana met them in the hallway, not waiting to be asked for an update. "She's sleeping. The doctor says it's a bad ear infection. She may need surgery to have tubes put in."

Tears sprang to Hattie's eyes, a reaction to fatigue and the thought of having her small baby put to sleep.

Luc put his arm around her. "We'll deal with that when the time comes. Thank you, Ana. Hattie and I will take it from here. You go get some rest."

"If you're sure. I wrote down her medication schedule on the nightstand in her room and the two bottles are there, too."

In the nursery, Hattie approached the crib on tiptoe. But Deedee was sleeping peacefully, her bottom in the air as she crouched in a ball on the mattress.

Luc touched Hattie's arm. "I'll bring our bags up. Why don't you get ready for bed?"

Hattie couldn't resist stroking the baby's back. "She still feels so hot."

"The antibiotic will take a while to kick in. We can set the alarm and give her ibuprofen during the night. Go on," he urged. "You're weaving on your feet."

"Okay." Hattie took a quick shower and changed into a nightgown that was pretty but not overtly sexy. Now that they were home, her thoughts were in turmoil. She hated that she felt like an insecure teenager again, wondering if a boy liked her. Everything had seemed so simple, so natural out on the island.

But now…back on Luc's home turf, all her earlier reservations returned. Would Luc expect to share her room? Was she supposed to go to his?

The nursery was adjacent to Hattie's suite. Ana and Sherman had slept in a nearby guest room while Luc and Hattie were gone.

When Hattie returned to the baby's room, her steps faltered. She hung back in the hall, her heart wrenching painfully. In the room decorated with nursery rhyme murals, a night-light cast a soft, pink glow. Sitting in the maple rocker, his head leaned back, eyes half-closed, was Luc. And in his arms lay a sleeping baby.

Deedee was nestled against Luc's chest, one

tiny hand clutching a fold of his shirt. The contrast between the big strong male and the tiny helpless baby twisted something deep in Hattie's chest. This was what Leo had feared. That Luc would fall in love with Deedee.

Luc himself had alluded to the fact that he understood the bond between parent and child. Clearly Hattie's niece had wormed her way into his heart. Seeing the two people Hattie loved most in the world…seeing them like this made her realize that she had backed herself into a difficult, if not impossible, corner.

Luc didn't believe in romantic love anymore. And Hattie alone was responsible for his cynicism. But if he loved Deedee, how could she take the baby away when the time came? How could she break Luc's heart a second time?

In the dimly lit room, Luc crooned a soft lullaby, his pleasing baritone singing of diamond rings and mockingbirds. The tender way he held the baby was poignant.

Hattie made herself step into the room. "I'll take her now so you can get cleaned up."

Luc's eyes, sleepy lidded, surveyed his wife. "Are you coming to my room to sleep?"

Wow. Trust Luc to cut straight to the chase. She steadied herself with a hand on the dresser. His meaning was crystal clear. But she had no clue how to respond. "Well, uh…"

His expression went blank, no trace of anything revealed on his classically sculpted features. "Don't sweat it, Hattie. We're both tired. But I'll be more than happy to help with the baby during the night if you need a hand."

Before Hattie could come up with words to explain the confusion in her heart, Luc gently placed Deedee in the crib, brushed by Hattie, and was gone.

Hattie rubbed her eyes with the heels of her hands, inhaling deeply. *Damn it*. Had she hurt his feelings? His male pride? She hadn't intended to say no to sleeping with him, but his artless question caught her off guard. This was uncharted territory.

They could no longer use a pretend honeymoon as an excuse to indulge in passionate sex. They were once again smack-dab in the throes of reality. Luc had married Hattie because she asked him to help protect an innocent baby. And perhaps because he could make Hattie dance to his tune and prove that she meant nothing to him. Did he also expect their physical intimacy to continue?

The baby was sleeping peacefully. Hattie made sure the volume on the monitor was adjusted and slipped out of the room, pulling the door shut as she left. Her big bed, which had seemed so luxurious and comfortable last week, was now a torture device. She tossed and turned, flipping the covers back in an effort to get cool.

She missed Luc, missed his big strong body snuggling with hers. What did he want from her? He'd seemed completely calm during their earlier conversation...not that it was much of a conversation. He'd taken her momentary confusion as a "no," and Hattie hadn't meant that at all, at least not completely.

Her befuddled brain had been scrambling to process all the pros and cons of maintaining a sexual relationship now that they were home. Ana and Sherman would know...and Leo, probably. Something like that was difficult to keep a secret.

So when the situation with Eddie was resolved and Hattie had to go, what then?

* * *

The next morning, Deedee was noticeably im-
proved. Luc played with her for a half hour before
announcing he was going to the office.

Hattie handed the baby off to Ana and frowned
as she followed Luc down to the foyer. "You're
still supposed to be on your honeymoon. They
won't be expecting you…"

He shrugged into an immaculately tailored
navy suit jacket, his expression impassive. "I'm
back. Work will have piled up. I might as well
get a jump start on things."

Hattie couldn't think of a thing to say to stop
him from walking out the door.

As she stood at the window watching her husband's car move down the driveway, her cell
phone rang. After ascertaining that it was an
unknown number, she answered. "Hello."

"Mrs. Cavallo?"

"Yes."

"This is Harvey Sharpton. I work for your husband, and I have good news."

Hattie's chest tightened. "What is it? Tell me,
please."

"Little Deedee's father has screwed up royally

this time. Another DUI. A hit-and-run again, this time involving pedestrians. Fortunately, no one was fatally injured, but the judge threw the book at him. And when we came forward with the nurse's testimony, the one who heard Angela's request, the judge granted you sole custody."

Hattie could barely speak. "Thank you so much," she croaked.

"There are some papers you need to sign."

"I'll call you and make an appointment soon. I appreciate your calling me."

She sank down on the bottom step of the grand, sweeping staircase and put her face in her hands. The relief was overwhelming. She wanted to tell Luc immediately…needed to share her joy with the one person who would understand more than anyone else. But he was gone.

All day she rehearsed what she would say. Forty-eight hours ago, it would have been much easier. The Luc she had made love to on her honeymoon was far more approachable than the stern businessman he had reverted to upon their return.

When he didn't make it home in time for dinner, her stomach sank. Maybe she was foolishly naive. Building castles in the air instead of planning for a future without Luc.

Finally, at eleven o'clock, she went to bed and fell into a fitful sleep. Something awoke her in the wee hours—a muffled thud, perhaps a door closing. She glanced at the clock on the bedside table. It was already time to give the baby a dose of medicine. Without bothering to put on a robe, she stole down the hall in her bare feet and opened the nursery door. For the second time, she found Luc with Deedee in his arms. He was standing beside the bed, the infant on his shoulder, patting her softly on the back.

Luc was wearing nothing but thin cotton boxers. Despite the hour and her fatigue, Hattie's body responded. It was conditioned now to expect searing pleasure, and Luc's scent, his masculine beauty, triggered all sorts of dancing hormones.

He turned to face her, speaking softly. "I've already given her the medicine. I thought you were asleep."

She shrugged. "I had a lot on my mind."

Ignoring Hattie's conversational gambit, Luc kissed Deedee's head before laying her back in the bed. He yawned and stretched, the corded muscles in his arms and chest flexing and rippling. "I checked her temp. It's almost normal. You don't need to worry."

Deedee wasn't Hattie's greatest concern at the moment. Instead, it was the way Luc was acting…aloof, unconcerned—about Hattie, that is. She took a step closer to him. "I never meant to imply that I wasn't going to sleep with you. You caught me by surprise, that's all. Do you want me to come with you now? I'm glad you're home."

He stilled, his dark eyes opaque, impossible to read. His shrug spoke volumes. "The baby needs you."

And I don't.

The unspoken words hovered between them. They might as well have been an aerial banner tugged through the sky by a plane.

Hattie didn't know what to say. It seemed as if he was trying purposefully to hurt her. And he was succeeding.

But she had learned a lot about him in the last week. Deep inside the coldly confident, unemotional man was a younger Luc. One who had been hurt repeatedly. One who had learned to shield his softer side. One who built walls. She took a courageous step in his direction. "The reason I wasn't able to sleep is because you weren't beside me."

Luc teetered on the edge of his own personal hell. Hattie was offering herself to him, coming to him of her own free will.

He was almost positive she was falling in love with him. Women couldn't hide things like that. Hattie didn't sleep around. And even though he was her husband, she wouldn't have shared his bed just for sex.

So why was he hesitating?

The dark knot of remembered pain inside him said, *Do it. Tell her to go to hell. Tell her you don't need a wife who's been bought and paid for. Tell her you don't want her.*

Would she see through the lie?

Could he instead reach for the rosy future that seemed almost within his grasp? A wife, a baby, a happily-ever-after?

People he loved left him. His parents. Hattie. If he brought her and the baby into his heart and home and then lost them, he wasn't sure he'd survive.

He clenched his fists, fighting the urge to grab her and pull her close. Instead, he shrugged. "We should probably reevaluate our relationship. See where things stand with the custody situation. I have a hell of a lot to catch up on at work…and you'll be spending time with the baby."

Hattie's face went white, her expression agonized. "So you were just using me in Key West because I was convenient?"

"Don't cast me as the villain in this drama," he said roughly. Sexual desire and searing regret choked him. "If anything, we used each other. You were wet and willing."

"You're a selfish ass," she said, tears choking her voice and welling in her beautiful eyes.

"I gave you what you wanted. You and the baby are safe. Don't ask for the moon, Hattie."

Eighteen

Don't ask for the moon, Hattie. The careless words jangled in her head. She barely slept at all, and when dawn broke, she knew what she had to do. It would have to be a covert operation. Ana and Sherman couldn't be caught in the middle.

Breakfast was miserable. Despite Deedee's chortling happiness, Luc and Hattie barely spoke, concentrating on brief exchanges of information that left her grieving and heartsick.

By ten o'clock the house was empty. Ana and Sherman had gone to the market. Patti was back at school. Luc was at the office. As soon as Deedee went down for her morning nap, Hattie started packing. She walked the hallways back and forth, barely able to concentrate, her skin cold as ice. The pain was crushing. When the suitcases were in the car, she fled. Out the door, down the steps, the baby clasped to her chest.

Luc had sent Hattie's clunker car into the shop for an overhaul. The stylish new minivan that she was still learning to drive was backed into the garage. She snapped Deedee into the car seat, hands shaking, jumped into the driver's seat, put the car in gear and tore out of the driveway.

She drove on autopilot, her heart bleeding. Luc would never love her again. She had killed those feelings in him. He wanted her body, but with his iron control, he was clearly able to deny them even that.

If she stayed in his house an hour more, she might be reduced to begging. And Luc didn't deserve that. He had helped her when she needed it most, but that reason no longer existed. She and Deedee were on their own.

The miles flashed by as she cruised the interstate. Where would she go? What was the next step? She had credit cards galore, but what if Luc disabled them in order to force her home?

Hastily, she did a mental accounting of the cash

in her purse…maybe four hundred dollars at the most. That wouldn't last long. But she had to go someplace where no one could find her. At least until she figured out what she was going to do.

Luc leaned back in his office chair and rubbed his neck. He had a killer headache. Thank God Leo was coming over for dinner tonight. His company would be a welcome diversion from the stilted, overly polite conversation to which he and Hattie had been reduced.

For the first time since the honeymoon, Luc arrived home at five-thirty. Leo was not far behind him.

Luc's brother wore a rumpled suit and offered a rueful apology. "Sorry for arriving unfashionably early. But I had a meeting in this part of town, and it didn't seem worth driving back to the office at rush hour."

Luc led him into the library and poured them each a finger of whiskey. "No worries. Deedee is starting to pull up on things, so Ana says she thinks Hattie and the baby went shoe shopping. They're not even back yet. We've got time to relax before dinner."

Leo settled his large frame into a spacious easy chair. After downing his drink in one gulp, he sighed, closed his eyes and spoke. "How are the two of you getting along?"

"No problems." Luc paced restlessly.

"Do you love her?"

"Who are you? Dr. Ruth? I'm not sure what love is."

"Then why did you marry her? Our lawyers have the ability to make mincemeat out of old Eddie. Tying the knot was totally unnecessary. So why did you do it?"

Luc had asked himself that same question a hundred times. The answer was clear, but it was too soon to tell his brother. Leo's propensity for mischief shouldn't be underestimated.

"It was the right thing to do. Protecting the baby."

"I'll give you that. You always did love playing the hero. But there's got to be more."

Sherman appeared in the door. "Excuse me, Mr. Luc. Ana found this note with your name on it. It was on the desk in the kitchen."

Luc ripped open the envelope and stared at the words without comprehension.

Leo came to stand beside him. "What is it? What's wrong?"

Luc had never been as scared as he was at this moment. "She's gone. She has custody, and she's gone."

His brother snatched the piece of paper and scanned it rapidly, cursing beneath his breath. "We'll find her. She can't have gone far."

But they didn't. One day passed. Then two. Then three. Hattie's cell phone was turned off, so the GPS locator was useless. None of her credit cards showed any sign of activity. It was as if she and Deedee had vanished off the face of the earth.

Luc was surviving on black coffee and three hours of sleep a night. His frustration with the police was enormous, but even he had to admit that there was no indication of foul play.

Hattie had left of her own free will. And she had taken his heart with her, dragging it in the wake of the speeding car, shredding it as the miles passed.

Leo was a rock. He moved in, and between the two of them, they hired the best detectives their considerable fortune could buy. But the P.I. reports were little comfort. When a person wanted to disappear, it could take weeks, months to track them down.

Luc lay in bed, night after night, dry-eyed, his body ice-cold. Pride. Injured pride had caused this debacle. All he'd had to do was tell Hattie he loved her more than life. Assure her that he had no plans to ever be parted from her or from Deedee.

If the lawyer had managed to give the news to Luc first instead of Hattie, Luc could have been prepared. But Luc had been too damn busy to listen to his voice mails.

On the fourth day, he caught a break. In her haste, Hattie had left behind the baby's antibiotic. Since Deedee had only been taking it a few days, there was a good chance the child's infection would return without the whole course of treatment.

Once Luc realized the omission, the detectives started monitoring the pediatrician's office with the cooperation of the doctor who was a friend of Luc's. At two-thirty in the afternoon of the fifth miserable day, a call came in requesting a replacement refill.

Luc practically grabbed the detective by the throat. "Tell me you got some information."

The grizzled sixtysomething veteran nodded, his gaze sympathetic. "The call originated from a Motel 6 in Marietta. Here's the address."

Hattie walked the floor, trying to soothe the cranky infant. Based on the last time she'd started the medicine, Deedee might not feel any better until at least forty-eight hours had passed.

Right after the honeymoon when the baby was ill, Hattie had been backed up with Luc's help and support. Now she was completely alone. The feelings of desolation and heartbreak were too much to bear. Her psyche adapted by shutting down all of Hattie's emotional pain sensors.

She was calm, too calm, but the unnatural state enabled her to function.

She had finally gotten Deedee to sleep late in the afternoon and had slumped onto the adjoining bed, craving a nap, when a loud knock hammered on the door of Room 106. Thankfully, the baby was dead asleep and didn't even stir.

Hattie peered through the peephole. *Dear God. Luc.* She wrung her hands, her brain paralyzed.

His distinctive voice sounded through the thin wood. "I see the car. I know you're in there. Open up, damn it."

Like a robot, she twisted the lock and turned the knob. As she stepped back into the room, Luc blew in with a barrage of rain and wind. A storm was brewing, the skies dark and boiling with clouds.

They faced off in the boxlike room.

He was haggard and pale, his shirt wrinkled, his hair a mess. Nothing about him suggested a successful entrepreneur.

Her heart iced over as the recollection of his deliberate cruelty flooded back.

"What do you want, Luc?" Fatigue enveloped her. She turned her back on him deliberately, sitting on the nearest bed and scooting back against the headboard. She pulled her knees to her chest, arms wrapped protectively around them.

His eyes were dark with misery. "I want *you.*"

"Liar." She said it without inflection, but she saw him flinch as the insult found its mark.

He shrugged out of his jacket and swiped a

hand through his wet hair. Thunder boomed, and the lights flickered. "I made a mistake. I was afraid to tell you how I felt. I never meant to drive you away."

Her fingernails dug into her legs. "I'm not stupid, Luc. I realized early on that one reason you agreed to help me was so that you could control things. You wanted the power this time. Lucky you. It worked."

He took a step toward the bed, but she stopped him with an outstretched arm.

Frustration carved grooves into his handsome face. "That idea lasted for about ten minutes. I told myself I wanted to hurt you...like you had hurt me. But I was kidding myself. I didn't want you to leave, Hattie."

"The lawyer called me. Eddie's not a threat anymore."

"I know. I read your note. It's wonderful news, but I'd rather have heard it from you face-to-face."

"You can give me part of that settlement now," she said calmly, her heart coming to life so that it could shatter into a million painful pieces. "We don't need your help anymore. We don't need you."

The look in his eyes made her ashamed. Spitefulness was not in her nature, but the need to lash out was inescapable.

He sat down at the foot of the bed, close enough for her to smell his aftershave and his natural, masculine scent. His eyes were dark, but no darker than the shadows beneath them. And he hadn't shaved. The anomaly disturbed her.

He touched her knee. A brief flash of heat tried to warm her, but he took his hand away. "What if *I* need *you?*" he asked hoarsely.

Hope flared in her chest. She smashed it ruthlessly. "You can buy anything you need."

The tired, wry twist of his lips was painful to watch. "I'm pretty sure you believed that ten years ago. It wasn't true then, and it isn't true now. My money doesn't give me control over you, Hattie. You're the one with all the power in this relationship."

"I'm a single, homeless mom with no job."

Again he winced. "You have a home," he said quietly. "And a husband who loves you more than life."

A single tear found its way down her cheek. "You never told me. Not once. We had sex a dozen times, maybe more…but you treated it like recreation. Not at all like love. And I know that's my fault. I'm sorry, Luc. Sorry I treated your love so callously back then."

He bowed his head briefly. "I should have said the words you needed to hear. But I was scared," he said. "You had the power to destroy me, Hattie. You still do."

Her lips trembled. "You've played games with my feelings. You hate me for what I did to you."

"I *tried* to hate you," he said softly. "For years. But it didn't work. When you showed up in my office that day, it was as if life had given me another chance. For a very short while, I told myself it was revenge I wanted. But I lied even to myself, Hattie. I loved you. I love you. I don't think I ever really stopped loving you. You have to believe me."

"Or what?"

"Or I'm going to buy this motel and lock you in this room until you come to your senses and admit you love me, too."

Hattie was shaking so hard, she was afraid

she might fly apart. She wanted so badly to be certain he was telling the truth. "I don't want a relationship where both of us are jockeying for control. I don't want to play mind games. I need to be in an equal partnership. If I decide to go back to my career when Deedee starts school, I don't want any flack about that just because you're too rich for your own good. I'll dress up for parties and I'll hostess for you, but I may still clip the occasional coupon..." She ran out of breath.

"Is that all?"

"Isn't that enough?"

"I'll let you make all the decisions from now on."

"Liar." This time she said it with rueful humor.

He leaned forward and found her mouth in a kiss so exquisitely tender it thawed the block of ice in her chest. Tears trickled down her cheeks, but he kissed them away. He took her face in his hands, his expression grave. "I love you, Hattie Parker."

Her lips trembled. Her arms went around his neck in a stranglehold. "I love you, Luc Cavallo.

And remember…my name isn't Parker anymore. I belong to you."

She felt the mighty shudder that racked his body, struggled to breathe as his arms crushed her in an unbreakable grip.

"Have you forgiven me?" she asked quietly, still feeling the sting of regret. "I cost us so much time."

He pulled back to look her in the eyes, his own deadly serious. "Maybe we both needed to grow up. Maybe we needed to be the people we are now so we could love Deedee as our own."

She sniffled, having a hard time with the juxta-position of soaring happiness and recent despair. "Take me home, Luc. Take *us* home."

He tucked her head beneath his chin, their heartbeats thudding in unison. "I thought you'd never ask."

Epilogue

Five months later, in a small villa in the south of France, Hattie caught her breath as her husband's rigid length entered her slowly. The sensation was exquisite.

His breathing was labored, his face flushed. He loved her gently, as he had in recent weeks.

She wrapped her legs around his waist and squeezed. "I won't break," she complained.

Late-afternoon shadows painted their nude bodies with warm light. In a nearby cheval mirror, she watched as he penetrated her with a lazy rhythm. The tantalizing pace sent her soaring. He waited until her peak receded slowly and then found his own release.

Afterward, Luc ran his hand over the small bump where her flat stomach used to be. They had made a baby that very first time in Key West. A fact that Luc continually referred to with pride.

He nuzzled her belly. "I think he's a boy." Their ultrasound was scheduled soon.

She sighed, feeling sated and content. "We're going to have our hands full with two little ones so close together."

"We have Ana and Sherman to help. We'll be fine."

She brushed a lock of dark hair from his forehead. "You're my knight in shining armor. You rescued Deedee and me. I'll never forget it."

Luc rolled to his back, taking her with him to sprawl on his chest. His eyes were alight with happiness. "You've got it all wrong, my love. The two of you rescued me."

* * * * *